PRAISE FOR THE NOVELS OF KEITH RAFFEL

A FINE AND DANGEROUS SEASON

"A compelling story, written with a sure hand, that keeps you intrigued. But watch out for the gut punches. They come often and unexpectedly. Raffel definitely has his game on."—**Steve Berry, author of** *The King's Deception*

"A rare historical novel—exciting and utterly believable—with Jack Kennedy as you've never seen him. Raffel is a master storyteller. I loved *A Fine and Dangerous Season*."—**Gayle Lynds, author of** *The Book of Spies*

"It's been half a century since the Cuban Missile Crisis brought us to the edge of the abyss. It's about time we got a page-turning thriller this good about it. The stakes are incredibly high, the action swift and chilling, the writing sleek and smooth. And the historical characters, from JFK to General Curtis LeMay, leap off the page. It may be fiction, but you'll believe every word of it."—**William Martin, author of** *The Lincoln Letter*

"Think you know JFK? Think again. Keith Raffel's novel *A Fine and Dangerous Season* is a nail-biting, meticulously researched foray into the real-life thriller territory of the Cuban Missile Crisis. Don't miss it!"—**Kelli Stanley, author of** *City of Secrets*

"Raffel takes the reader on a wild ride from Stanford University right before World War II to one of the most dangerous moments of the Cold War. Loved it!"—**Rebecca Cantrell, author of** *A City of Broken Glass*

"A clever and deftly crafted retelling of the Cuban Missile Crisis through the eyes of JFK's old Stanford buddy. Not to be missed."—**Robert Gregory Browne, author of the** *Trial Junkies* **series**

"What I find impressive and captivating about this book is the philosophy, the symbolism and the poetry with which Raffel writes. I think this book … is destined to become a movie. I will be first in line to see it."—*Examiner.com*

DOT DEAD
"A murder mystery worthy of a Steve Jobs keynote presentation."
—*New York Times*

"A fast-paced, truly witty mystery set in the maze and madness of Silicon Valley … A fun read."—**Stuart M. Kaminsky, Grand Master Award-winning mystery author**

"Keith Raffel, an entrepreneur who sold his CRM firm, UpShot, to Siebel Systems … publishes a surprisingly entertaining whodunit."—*Inc. Magazine*

"Raffel, founder of a software company, has written a well-plotted mystery with … action and plot twists … You can't go wrong."—*Library Journal*

"This book is a pleasure, and especially fun to read about Palo Alto from a person who grew up there."—*San Jose Mercury*

SMASHER

"Take a taut roller coaster ride in *Smasher* behind Silicon Valley's doors: takeover bids, nail biting deals, a hidden story of physics and heart. Crisp and atmospheric I couldn't put it down. Hold on and prepare to stay up all night."—**Cara Black, author of the bestselling Aimée Leduc series**

"Keith Raffel is an incredibly engaging writer. *Smasher* swings seamlessly from the cut-throat maneuverings of Silicon Valley to the equally competitive world of particle physics, and yet Raffel never forgets that this is a story about people. A smart, humane, compelling read."—**Marcus Sakey, author of *Brilliance***

"Raffel blends computer world wheeling and dealing with the academic world's lust for glory and fame in his compelling second mystery to feature Silicon Valley entrepreneur Ian Michaels." —***Publisher's Weekly***

"The author, founder of an Internet software company … excels at showing his characters' humanity. Raffel briskly moves Smasher from the callousness of Silicon Valley … to the equally cutthroat world of academia."—***Mystery Scene Magazine***

"If the proof of the author is in the second novel, Raffel delivers with his new mystery, *Smasher*, set in the convoluted corridors of Silicon Valley power."—***Palo Alto Weekly***

"Keith Raffel, himself a successful Silicon Valley entrepreneur, has made good use of his knowledge and experience to produce an intelligent mystery story that will undoubtedly have a broad appeal."—***Jewish Post and Opinion***

A Fine and
DANGEROUS
SEASON

Other novels by Keith Raffel

Dot Dead: A Silicon Valley Mystery

Smasher: A Silicon Valley Thriller

Drop By Drop: A Thriller

KEITH RAFFEL

A Fine and
DANGEROUS
SEASON

A NOVEL

THOMAS & MERCER

Published by Thomas & Mercer, Seattle
www.apub.com

Amazon, the Amazon logo, and Thomas & Mercer are trademarks of Amazon .com, Inc., or its affiliates.

ISBN-13: 9781477818206
ISBN-10: 1477818200

Cover design by Dale Roberts and Travis Young

Library of Congress Control Number: 2013919653

Printed in the United States of America

To my brothers Corey and Wes and my sister Dena

"October is a fine and dangerous season
in America."

Thomas Merton

PART ONE

Chapter One
October 24, 1962
Palo Alto, California

I put down the slide rule and hoisted up the black handset.

"Yeah?" It was too early in the morning for my phone manners to have kicked in.

"Am I speaking to Nathan Michaels?" the caller asked in a New England twang.

I hesitated for a moment. "Jack? Can that be you?"

"No, it's not Jack. It's his brother Robert."

By his second word, I'd realized my mistake. The pitch was too high, the tone too reedy to be Jack. And why would he be calling me more than two decades after we'd last seen each other?

"Mr. Attorney General, I am sorry. What can I do for you?"

I wouldn't have tried to be polite to Jack, but Bobby, well, I'd never met him, and he *was* head of the Justice Department — even if his appointment could be attributed to bloodlines rather than achievement.

"The president, uh, needs to see you," he said.

"I don't mean to be rude, but I don't want to see *him*."

"And I don't mean to be rude, but I don't believe you."

"What? I really don't want to see him," I repeated.

"I meant it sounds like you *did* mean to be rude."

I snorted. "Okay, maybe I did."

"Listen, this is no social call. You were in the War. Your commander-in-chief has asked to see you."

"I left the service in '45."

"My brother needs to see you right away," he insisted.

"Isn't he a little busy right now?"

⌣

He had been on television the night before last. The Russians had moved missiles into Cuba. Yesterday my twin sons had come home with stories of air raid drills which, as best I could tell, consisted of ducking under their desks at Palo Alto High School. Ten pounds of wood and steel didn't offer much protection against a 20-megaton warhead air-mailed C.O.D. from Siberia. And our little piece of paradise in Palo Alto would be a target or at least close to one. The Navy's P-2 Neptune sub hunters flew out of Moffett Field a few miles down the freeway.

"Mr. Michaels, uh, you're called Nate, aren't you?"

"Yes," I said, noting he hadn't actually asked permission to call me by my first name.

"Well, Nate, President Kennedy is busy and so am I and that means I don't have time to fuck around with you and neither does he."

When I woke her, my wife clung to me and asked me not to go, said that no good would come of it. But ninety minutes after I hung up the phone, I was flying back to Washington on an Air Force T-39 that had been waiting for me at Moffett Field.

Chapter Two

What with a refueling stop, a forty-five minute drive into the city from Andrews Air Base, and a three-hour time change, it was seven in the evening when the guard at the White House gate waved through the Air Force car I was riding in.

A little sparrow of a woman with a nest of brown hair and rimless glasses was waiting for me at the side door.

"Follow me, Mr. Michaels."

Carrying an athletic bag that held two changes of underwear, a couple of white button-downs, a razor, a pair of pajamas, and a copy of *Seven Days in May*, I did as instructed. After racking my brain in the airspace above California, Nevada, and Idaho over why I'd been summoned, I stopped wondering while gazing down on the purple peaks of Wyoming. Now I concentrated on keeping up with my guide as we trotted through a maze of hallways and a warren of offices. She stopped in front of a huge set of white wooden doors, knocked, and twisted the brass knob without waiting for an answer. Leaning her torso around the half-opened door, she chirped, "I have Mr. Michaels here."

"Bring him in, Mrs. Lincoln," said the familiar voice.

She swung the door all the way open and I entered.

John Fitzgerald Kennedy, former friend and current president, sat in a rocking chair outfitted with cloth padding. I'd read it was good for his back. To his right was a couch seating three and to his left were nine weighty wooden chairs, all filled with advisors and cabinet secretaries recognizable from NBC's *Huntley-Brinkley Report* and the news pages of *The San Francisco Chronicle*. They were staring right back at me.

The attorney general rose and said, "Let's give the president and Mr. Michaels some time. We all have plenty to do."

Out filed the dozen officials. Bobby Kennedy reached to shake and I transferred the bag to my left hand. As he grasped my right hand, he searched my face for an answer, but I didn't even know the question. General Maxwell Taylor, whose uniform jacket provided a backdrop for a kaleidoscopic exhibition of ribbons, introduced himself. A man I recognized as John McCone, head of the CIA, scowled as he went by. Dean Rusk, Robert McNamara, and the others trudged out without even a glance my way.

For the first time in twenty-two years, I was looking at Jack Kennedy in person. He was returning my stare, leaning forward on his rocker. His face had filled out – no, more than filled out, it had puffed up. The blue-gray smudges under his eyes contrasted with the orangey tan of the rest of his face.

I heard the door click shut behind me.

"Long time, Nate. You look good."

He held out his hand from the rocker, and I took it without thinking. His grasp was firm, keen, still powerful. I'd read that the custom of shaking hands had arisen to show that you held no weapon and hence that you came in friendship. I flexed my fingers and let my hand drop.

"My father used to say the three ages of man were young, middle-aged, and 'you look good,'" I said.

He laughed. "Wise man, your dad."

"You, on the other hand, look like shit," I said.

"I've had a rough couple of weeks," Kennedy said. "You know, I figured you'd come. You were always a little impetuous. Always ready for a quick getaway."

He smiled. It didn't take any willpower at all to refrain from smiling back.

"I never thought of myself as all that impetuous," I said.

His chin cupped in his right hand, Kennedy began to rock a little. "I don't think people change much. Remember the train ride we took down to L.A. when you should have been studying? What about your road trip up to Canada?"

Right after the last time I'd seen him, I'd thrown some clothes in a suitcase and driven nonstop up the Pacific Coast to Vancouver. Two days later I managed to parlay my summer flying lessons and pilot license into a commission in the Royal Canadian Air Force and by the end of the month was enrolled in the Commonwealth Empire Air Training Scheme.

"I was tired of waiting for war to come. I got a jump on things. But then, didn't you enlist right after me?"

"I tried, but failed the army physical."

"Your back?"

"Among other things."

"But the Navy took you."

"Eventually," he agreed. "Um, about what happened, I'm sor...."

That did it. The wall of self-control I'd built brick by brick during the flight across the country came tumbling down. I took a step toward him. "Listen, I can't even begin to guess why you've hauled me out here from California, but I never, and I mean never, want to talk about what happened all those years ago. Bring it up and I'm back in Palo Alto. The whole world can blow up for all I care."

He looked up at me from his chair and said, in a soft voice, "That was before the War, Nate. In the distant past. Isn't that too long to nurse a grudge?"

"Probably," I said. "Consider it a character defect."

He breathed out and moved on. "All right," he said and rubbed his hands together. "Let's see how much you do care about the world blowing up. Have a seat."

"I'll stand," I said and tightened my fingers around the handle of my bag.

"Have it your way." He didn't seem fazed, but then he must have acquired a fair amount of experience dealing with stubborn and opinionated people in the twenty-one months of his presidency. "Any trouble getting away?" he asked.

"No." My wife *really* hadn't wanted me to go. I'd called my secretary Karen at home and winced when I heard her swear for the first time in the three years we'd worked together. She was right – with only a week to go before the end of our fiscal year at Hewlett-Packard, the timing was not good for a jaunt to Washington, no matter who was asking. I was supposed to be meeting with Douglas Aircraft in Long Beach the day after tomorrow to close a big sale. I left it to Karen to convince Bill or Dave to go for me. The last thing I did before leaving the house was to look in on the twins. I spent half a minute watching their backs rise and fall with the deep, guileless sleep of overactive teenage boys.

"As long as you're up, would you turn on the TV?" Kennedy asked. I walked over to the set sunk into the wall and did as I was asked. "CBS has a special report on."

We said nothing while the tube warmed up. When the picture did appear, a man against a background of the Pentagon, identified by subtitle as Charles von Freund, was saying, "Everybody's lips are sealed. We are under what amounts to a wartime censorship program. Back to you, Walter."

Like the president, Walter Cronkite, the man who'd replaced Douglas Edwards a few months ago as anchor on the *CBS Evening News*, sported dark smudges under his eyes. "There is not a great deal of optimism tonight," he intoned.

Kennedy's right hand moved in a chopping motion. "Enough."

I flicked the switch off, straightened up, and asked, "Why am I here again?"

"You have a good war record." He opened a manila folder on his desk and started reading. "Captain Michaels displayed extraordinary...."

I cut him off. "That was a long time ago."

"Yeah, October, '43. The citation is signed 'by command of General Doolittle.' With that Distinguished Service Cross you could have stayed in the service."

"I'm just a business executive out in California now."

"I wonder why you weren't called up for Korea."

"I guess they needed hotshot fighter pilots qualified for jets, not old B-17 pilots."

"Serving your country is behind you now?"

Yeah, it was. I'd been running away from my war experiences for seventeen years. I'd had enough. I didn't tell Kennedy that, though.

He pulled out a sheaf of photographs and handed one of them over.

It was taken from a plane. I could see tiny figures on the ground along with heavy equipment and eight large cigar-shaped cylinders.

"These are?"

"U-2 photos of a Soviet missile installation in Cuba. You see that blockhouse over there?"

"Yeah."

"Well, there are nuclear warheads in there."

I dropped my bag and sat down.

"Are any of those missiles ready?"

"Maybe, most likely, but in any case they're working hard to get them there. We've also spotted some IL-28 bombers that can carry nukes. If they're not combat-ready yet, they will be soon."

"How are the Soviets getting the warheads to Cuba?" I asked.

"By sea. Their ships will get to our naval cordon tomorrow. I've given orders to stop and search them. The Soviets say it will be an act of war."

"Do they mean it?"

"Doesn't much matter. It looks like I'm going to order air attacks and an invasion to take out the missile sites."

"And if the Soviets respond?"

"Then we will respond."

"By attacking the Soviet Union?" I asked. He nodded. "With nuclear weapons?"

"If they use them, we will have no choice."

I picked up my bag. "If I'm about to die, I'd rather be home with my family."

As the president rose, his lips tightened and eyes narrowed. His back had not gotten any better in the past two decades.

"Remember that Sunday when you took me up to your parents' for brunch?"

"Yes."

"The guy from the Soviet consulate who was there...."

"Maxim Volkov."

"Right. Do you know what he's doing now?" Kennedy asked, his face a few feet from mine.

"No. He's still alive?"

"Yeah."

"Good to know. I've wondered. My parents gave him a going-away party in 1942. They got a few letters from him, but heard nothing once the War was over. Dad figured he'd been purged."

"You were pretty good friends."

"Yeah, family friends," I said.

"Two months ago he came to Washington as a counselor in the Soviet Embassy here. McCone tells me the counselor job is a cover. He's KGB, the new head of Soviet intelligence here in the United States."

So Volkov *had* been using my father and me all those years ago. One more betrayal from those years before the War. "You were right about him, then," I said.

Kennedy didn't gloat. He kept on talking. "The CIA doesn't think it's a coincidence he came just as the missiles were being smuggled into Cuba."

"I appreciate the update on Volkov, but you didn't fly me across the country for that."

He shook his head. "In a meeting with our top Soviet expert at the State Department yesterday, Volkov mentioned you and your dad."

"Really?"

"He was the one who said you were good friends. Llewellyn Thompson, that's our expert, says Volkov was quite emphatic about wanting to see you again."

"You know my father died in '48?"

"Yeah, I'm sorry. He was a great man. Volkov knew he'd passed away. He meant he wished he could see *you*. He said you were his one friend in the United States."

"Okay. So he wants to see an old friend?"

"Come on, Nate. The KGB station chief meets with the State Department's top Russian expert and brings up your name for no good reason?"

"Because he knows we were friends."

"And he thinks he can trust you." Kennedy shook his head. "I want you to get in touch with him."

"What do I know about politics and diplomacy? I sell engineering instruments in California."

"Sometimes it's more important who a man is than what he knows."

"Maybe I've changed since 1940."

He shook his head. "I don't think so. Being president means putting bets down on people. No matter what happened between us, I know you have a good head on your shoulders, and your war record shows you are more than competent. I'm comfortable betting on you."

"But ...." I started.

He waved away my interruption. "Here's what I *am* uncomfortable with – figuring out why the Russkies think you'd be a better channel than an official one. Here's a guess – Khrushchev wants a direct channel to the White House, one that some powerful faction in the Kremlin who wants war doesn't know about."

I could ignore the flattery. It was political b.s. Still, I leaned even closer to him. "So what do you want me to do?"

"Talk to your old friend. Have a vodka together. And find out what it would take to get out of this mess. Just listen and come back and tell me what he says. That's all. Don't worry. I'm not counting on you to save the world."

"A good thing," I said.

"If there's nothing there, no harm done. All you've missed is selling a few more oscilloscopes."

I hadn't mentioned that I sold oscilloscopes.

"Do I need some kind of CIA briefing?" I asked.

"I'd rather the CIA didn't even know what you were up to. They don't appreciate amateurs getting in the way.

"Makes sense to me. They're pros. They must know what they're doing."

"Not always," Kennedy said with a wince. "Remember how well the pros did at the Bay of Pigs."

Three months into his presidency, CIA-sponsored forces, who were supposed to rally a popular overthrow of Castro's regime, had instead been routed on a Cuban beach.

"Good point, but do you really think Volkov will tell me something you don't know?"

He shook his head. "Nope. You're probably here for nothing. Still, if there's a one in a million chance that having you talk to Volkov will do some good, I've gotta take it."

What choice did I have? Kennedy was an expert angler. He'd used the fate of the country as bait. I'd bitten and he'd reeled me in. Like he'd known he would.

Chapter Three

"No, thank you. No pork," I said to the navy steward.

"*You're* keeping kosher now?" Kennedy asked.

I jutted out my chin. "Since my wedding."

The president sat at the head of the dining room table. On his right were his brother and Charlie Bartlett, a reporter for *The Chattanooga Times*, along with his wife Martha. I sat across from the Bartletts, and Bobby's wife Ethel sat between the president and me. Hand-painted wallpaper showing scenes from the early days of the American Revolution encircled the room and gave me the sense that we six diners were marooned in the middle of Boston Harbor.

Neither of the Kennedy brothers felt much like talking. Every few minutes they would glance at each other and nod as if communicating via telepathy. They let Bartlett and Ethel act as social Sherpas and carry the conversational burden. Bartlett told me Kennedy and his wife had first met at a party at his house.

He looked up and addressed our host. "And what did you do, Jack?" he asked.

"I leaned across the asparagus and asked Jackie for a date," Kennedy said in a voice that indicated he'd told the story many times, but it didn't seem to matter. Martha and Ethel both clapped their hands with delight.

I wondered where the president's wife was – of course, I'd never met her – but I wasn't going to ask. I wanted to keep both Kennedy's and my personal lives out of all this.

Bobby introduced me to Ethel as one of his brother's best friends from before the War. I was being treated like a long-time intimate, a role I had no interest in playing. I'd spent years pushing the couple of months I'd known Jack back into the locked box of my subconscious, and now he'd popped out again. I didn't want to be buddy-buddy with him. When I'd confronted him, I'd lost my temper. No need to go through that again. I'd have the meeting with Volkov and then fly back home.

No beauty, Ethel grew in attractiveness as she performed her assigned role as dinner party hostess. She flattered by focusing her attention on me. With charm and apparent interest, she managed to draw out all the essentials of my *curriculum vitae*: war veteran, married, twin boys, business executive, Palo Alto resident.

"Eunice, my sister-in-law, went to Stanford during the War and loved Palo Alto too," Ethel said. "She couldn't decide if it was paradise because of the weather or because it was so far from Boston."

As I smiled, I heard the door behind me swing open. The person entering the room was no steward.

"What is it, Mac?" the president asked.

The horn-rimmed glasses and high forehead served as badges of brainpower for the president's national security advisor, McGeorge Bundy.

"The navy says the Soviet ships have stopped before reaching our interdiction line," Bundy replied.

Bobby sighed like a bicycle tire that had just run over a tack, Ethel clapped, Bartlett raised his flute of white wine. "A toast," he said.

I grabbed my own crystal glass as did the others except for the president.

"What are we toasting?" he asked.

"That Soviet ships on their way to Cuba have turned around," Bartlett said.

The president shook his head. "You don't want to celebrate too early in this game."

Chapter Four

Lying on top of the bedcovers at half past midnight, I was a hundred and fifty pages into *Seven Days in May* when the knock came.

The door to my White House bedroom swung open before I said a thing.

I'd been reading by the light of a single lamp on the nightstand. Now in the backlit doorway, Kennedy stood, a shadowy figure. "I figured you'd be awake," he said.

"It's dark. Flick the switch," I said.

I brought my hand up to shield my eyes from the explosion of light. Kennedy shut the door.

I blinked a few times. He was wearing the same gray suit pants he'd had on earlier with a white undershirt and backless leather slippers. He needed a shave.

"I figured you'd be awake," he repeated. "In California it's not even ten yet."

"Couldn't sleep?" I asked.

"I *told* Bartlett it was too early to celebrate." He perched on the end of the bed and held up a long, curling sheet of light brown paper. While he ran his left hand back through his hair, he handed me the paper with his right.

Long lines of letters and numbers ran across the top of the paper, but I could decode that this message was addressed to my midnight visitor and had come in from Moscow minutes after we'd finished dinner. I unrolled the paper to see the bottom: "Respectfully yours, N. Khrushchev, First Secretary." I went back up to the top and started reading. The nitty-gritty started a few paragraphs down. I read aloud, "You, Mr. President, are not declaring quarantines, but advancing an ultimatum and threatening that unless we subordinate ourselves to your demands, you will use force."

"Keep going," Kennedy said.

I read silently for a minute and then recited:

The Soviet Government considers that violation of freedom of the use of international waters and international air space is an act of aggression, pushing mankind towards the abyss of a world missile-nuclear war. Consequently, the Soviet Government cannot give instructions to the captain of the Soviet vessels bound for Cuba to observe the instructions of the American naval forces blockading that island.

"That's enough," Kennedy said. "You've got the gist."

"And you're going to stop their ships," I said.

He ran that hand through his hair again. "Yeah."

"And then Khrushchev will retaliate with missiles?" I asked.

"I don't think he wants to. He was a commissar with the Red Army during the War. He must have seen tens of thousands of men killed with his own eyes. He can't want this."

"But?" I asked.

"I'm not sure he can stop it. And we can't leave those missiles in Cuba. General LeMay wants me to order a preemptive attack on Cuba and Russia now."

Curtis LeMay, the Air Force Chief of Staff, and a familiar name. Too familiar. "And what do you think?" I asked Kennedy.

"Maybe he's right. If a mugger puts his knife tip against your ribs, you can't tell him, 'Sure, just leave it there.'"

"So we *are* going have a nuclear war?" My left eye began to twitch as I thought of my family back in Palo Alto.

Kennedy was staring down at the intricate paisleys of the bedroom carpeting. "The odds favor it, but I want to give Khrushchev a last chance to get that knife out of my ribs. If we don't get the missiles out of Cuba – Mother of God – I'll be impeached. And if I were still a senator, I'd vote for conviction myself." He looked at the book that was folded open across my chest. "Or maybe it would be like in that book you're reading."

I tapped the cover with my finger. "*Seven Days in May* is fiction. No matter how much LeMay blusters in your meetings, the joint chiefs aren't going to stage a coup."

"No such luck."

Kennedy knew I was Jewish, but he was acting as though I were some kind of priest. What he was doing here was looking for sympathy – no, for absolution. I could give him none and said nothing.

"Good luck tomorrow with Volkov. See if there's a way to get the knife out of our ribs without blowing up the world."

He stood up and turned the overhead light back off. With the door open again, his outlined form said, "God bless."

Chapter Five

"So, all in all, how bad is it?" my wife asked.

I'd used the phone in my room to call home – why shouldn't the American taxpayer pay my long distance bill? – and the White House switchboard had put me through with no questions. It would be easy enough for someone to be monitoring the call, but I didn't give a damn.

"Well, they're muddling along," I said.

"It's me," she said. "You don't need to buoy me up."

She was right. *Muddling along* was putting a better face on the situation than it warranted.

"Okay, grasping at straws, then. It all seems unreal, detached. It's not like during the War. Then, you'd be shot at, you'd watch friends go down. They died one by one. They were mourned, missed."

"It wasn't like that for everyone." She was whispering so the boys wouldn't hear, but in all likelihood she didn't have to. It was ten thirty in Palo Alto and they would be in bed.

She'd lost aunts, uncles, and cousins to mass murder. After the War, her father had spent time and money looking for European cousins he'd never met. All gone.

"I know millions died during the War, but that was over years. Now you push a button and millions die in a day."

She hesitated before asking, "And President Kennedy, how is he handling things?"

She knew how I felt about him and why.

"On the surface, he seems cool and analytical, but I'm glad we have a president who fought in the War, who's seen men die up close. He doesn't want to push that button unless he has to."

"I'm not going to ask what you're doing, but the president thinks you can help?"

"He doubts it," I replied.

"But maybe?"

"One in a million, he said."

"He's lucky to have you there."

She had a lot more faith in me than I had in myself. Spousal loyalty, I guess. After we said good night, I put on my pajamas and turned off all the lights except for the one on the nightstand. I picked up *Seven Days in May*. I kept running my eyes over the same page, absorbing nothing until I fell asleep sometime after two.

Chapter Six

I reached over for my wife. When my fingers reached the far side of the bed unimpeded, I jerked up, realizing she wasn't there. My book tumbled to the floor.

What the hell was I doing here in a guestroom of the White House anyway? Was I still as impetuous as Kennedy says? Or was I just following orders like I did during the War?

After a shave and shower, I breakfasted with a fellow named Lem Billings, who occupied the guestroom next door to mine on the White House's third floor.

With a spoonful of oatmeal at mouth-level poised for delivery, Billings said, "Jack likes to have old friends around, people who knew him before he went into politics, people like you he can trust."

"What do you mean, *like me*?"

He swallowed and then sprinkled more brown sugar over his cereal. "Bobby's his brother. He's known him his whole life. He knows he can trust him. Me? I've known him since prep school. It does him good to have me around. I remember him mentioning you back in 1940."

"Mentioning me? Were you at Stanford too?"

"No, no. Mentioned in letters. We corresponded. I guess you were his best friend out West?"

"He wrote that?" I asked.

"Yeah, I think he did."

"It was a long time ago." Had I really been that close to the current proprietor of the White House? Bobby had said that last night. Hard to square with what had happened.

"Professor Morrison at Stanford told him you were one of the two or three brightest students he ever had," Billings went on. "Jack admires the way you joined the Canadian Air Force a year before Pearl Harbor. He even envies it. "

I guess it wasn't too hard for a millionaire-congressman-senator-president to keep track of someone. Was it the job of this Billings to do at breakfast what Ethel had done last night? Flatter me. Soften me up. Induce me to say yes to whatever Kennedy wanted?

The door swung open.

I stood up and Billings followed. "This is Harriet Collins," Billings said. "She's on the White House staff."

I shook a warm, pliable hand. "Pleased to meet you, Miss Collins."

I couldn't help staring for a moment. Miss Collins' hair was chestnut brown, her eyebrows dark, and – behind black-framed eyeglasses – her eyes sapphire blue. Her white blouse with a Peter Pan collar was tucked into a black skirt, but the modesty of her garb could not hide the precipitous inward curve that ran from her chest to her waist.

"Miss Collins graduated first in her class from Radcliffe last June," Billings said.

I shook free of her grip. "Congratulations," I said. My boys were sixteen. Miss Collins couldn't be more than six years older.

"Thank you."

Billings said, "Mrs. Lincoln asked Miss Collins to take care of any of your needs while you're here."

I wondered how I was going to get hold of Volkov. Maybe she could call the Russian Embassy? No, I'd walk. "Do you know where the Russian Embassy is?" I asked my newly assigned helpmate.

"Right up Sixteenth, past L," Miss Collins said. She tossed the ends of her pageboy haircut to point in what must have been a northerly direction.

"Thank you."

"That's it?" she asked.

"For now."

"I sit just outside Mrs. Lincoln's office. If you need anything at all, let me know."

"I will."

Chapter Seven

Of course, the White House was at 1600 Pennsylvania Avenue. That meant if Sixteenth Street had opted to cross Pennsylvania, it would have run right through the Oval Office. It hadn't, so at nine in the morning of October 25, fifteen minutes after my last swallow of oatmeal, I crossed Pennsylvania and followed a diagonal pathway through Lafayette Park.

I wore a black London Fog raincoat over my suit, not for protection against the rain – the day was sunny, breezy, and clear – but for warmth. The temperature here must have been thirty degrees lower than the mid-seventies we'd been enjoying back in Palo Alto. Then again, in Palo Alto, trees would only reluctantly shed their green and brown foliage after Thanksgiving, but here in the nation's capital the leaves' crimson and gold were already signaling their impending doom.

Waiting for the light to turn at K Street, I spotted what had to be the Russian Embassy a block and a half ahead. Antennas sprang from the gray mansion's roof like stalks in an Iowa cornfield. I didn't know what kind of clandestine signals were sneaking in or out from all that radio equipment, but I couldn't think of who would need it besides America's Cold War nemesis.

As I drew closer, the flapping hammer and sickle ensign over the front door confirmed my supposition. But no one stopped me from swinging open the wrought iron gate and walking to the oversized oak doors. In a dark foyer at the foot of a huge stone staircase, a woman not much older than Miss Collins sat behind a desk. She was even dressed in a white top and dark skirt like Miss Collins, but her appearance had been regimented by the Soviet State. Miss Collins exuded a soft pink femininity. This woman's sprayed mane looked more helmet than hairdo, her feline face shone with the iciness of northern steppes, and her breasts formed two cones as if tight-fitting armor were strapped on under that innocent blouse. Perhaps she was there to show walk-in traitors the harsh delights that awaited them in a workers' paradise.

"May I help you?" Her Russian accent didn't sound a lot different from Greta Garbo's in *Ninotchka*.

"I would like to speak to Comrade Volkov, please."

"Is he expecting you?"

"No. Maybe. I'm not sure. Perhaps you could check."

She swung her head to the side so she was looking at me sideways, with her left eye half-closed. "May I have your name, please?"

I told her. She dialed the phone and growled some words of Russian. So maybe she did think I was a spy off the street asking for a KGB man. I hope someone had told the FBI what I was up to. They must be keeping the embassy under surveillance. A perfect ending to my vacation in the nation's capital – being thrown in the federal pen at Leavenworth for espionage.

A stout man in a chocolate brown military uniform started stomping down the stone stairs with the assurance of a field officer, if not a general, but I couldn't figure out exactly what rank he was from the peculiar red and gold pips and stripes on his shoulder boards.

The New Woman began speaking into the receiver in a more respectful tone. Because of the approaching soldier or because of what she was hearing on the phone? She started scribbling something on a notepad even while giving a deferential nod to the soldier. She hung up the phone and looked up at me with a smile that conveyed all the warmth of her native land – assuming she'd been whelped in Siberia.

"He was expecting you after all, but is not in," she said. "He will meet you at the Occidental Restaurant at noon."

Chapter Eight

Among the dozens of politicians' photographs that lined the walls of the Occidental like Most Wanted posters at the post office, I spotted a young Harry Truman, an old Arthur Vandenberg, and an ageless Richard Nixon. I swung my eyes around to inspect the denizens of the other tables, all men in navy or gray. For all I knew, any one of them could be a senator or congressman or Supreme Court justice. Wait. A woman in a double-breasted red jacket was lifting a fork at a table at the other end of the dining hall. Hmm. She looked familiar. Well, she sure wasn't a senator – she was three decades too young to be Margaret Chase Smith. It would come to me. In the meantime her presence only accentuated the middle-aged masculinity of the room.

I looked down at my watch. In seconds the minute hand would hit the nine and my deadline of twelve forty-five would be reached. I wasn't anxious to go back to report to the White House that I hadn't seen Volkov. I turned back and checked the *maître d*'s station for a sign of him. I took a long pull on my iced tea and stared at a man's face made familiar by the television news. Who was it? The fingers of my memory were about to grasp the answer when I caught a familiar whiff of cologne, hair oil, and cigars. I was enfolded from behind in a Russian bear hug and my ears were accosted by a mighty roar of "Nathan." While I couldn't see Volkov myself, I watched the miscellany of congressmen and assistant secretaries turn their heads our way. Who would have thought a spy would want so much attention? Well, maybe he reckoned naked was the best disguise.

When Volkov's arms loosened for a moment, I turned to face him. His greased hair was thinner, his face more florid, his stomach more protuberant. If anything, he looked more Volkov than ever.

"I would say you look great, but I remember what your late father used to say," he said.

Volkov grabbed my cheeks between his meaty paws and gave me a sloppy kiss perilously close to my lips. He excused himself by saying, "We Russians are too sentimental." And then he went on, "You must miss your *otets*, your father."

"Every day."

"Me, as well. Those were great days before the War."

Twenty-two years after our last meal together, Volkov and I settled down for lunch. I was telling him about the twins, when he held his hand up like a traffic cop. "Wait. Come."

He raised himself from his chair and started wending his way between the tables, a Mack truck on a twisty country lane. There was nothing for it but to follow. He shook a hand about every other table. How could he be a spy if everyone knew him after such a short time in town?

He pulled up in front of the very table where the crimson-suited woman sat. It was her turn to be engulfed in the arms of the Russian bear. "Nancy," he roared this time.

The first name along with a closer look revealed the woman to be the chic Nancy Dickerson, who reported for CBS.

"Nancy, I would like for you to meet my old friend Nathan Michaels."

The reporter wriggled out of Volkov's hold and offered her hand.

"Mrs. Dickerson, I am a fan," I said.

She introduced us to her lunch companion, Harald – I didn't catch his last name – from the Norwegian embassy.

"And what do you do in this town, Mr. Michaels?" she asked me out of common courtesy.

"I'm visiting from California."

"Mr. Michaels is a school friend of President Kennedy," Volkov added.

"Is that right? Enjoy your stay, Mr. Michaels. And you, Maxim, enjoy your lunch."

The humorous lilt in her voice told me she'd seen Volkov sit down for a meal before.

Back at our table, I asked Volkov why he'd summoned me.

He reached across and touched my hand. "My friend, we have not seen each other since before Great Patriotic War. It is good to see you. That should be enough?"

"It is."

"Good. First food and drink, then business. I want to hear about your boys. They are wonderful, I am sure."

"They are. Do you have a family, Maxim?" I asked.

"No time," he said and sighed with regret, whether genuine or feigned I had no idea.

"Then I would like to hear about your career," I said.

"Fine, fine. You decide what you want for lunch while I go to gents'."

I had just decided on a hamburger when I heard, "Hello, Mr. Michaels."

I put down the bill of fare. Across from me in Volkov's vacated chair sat Mrs. Dickerson.

"I hope you don't mind," she said.

"And if I do?"

"Does your visit have anything to do with the Cuban crisis?" she asked me, silver mechanical pencil poised, social niceties forgotten.

"There's a crisis in Cuba?" I responded.

She laughed, but wasn't amused. "JFK is rallying the troops?"

"Troops? I wouldn't know. I'm an airman by trade."

She flashed her white teeth in a smile that I bet got her whatever she wanted nine times out of ten. "An airman? So he *is* thinking of bombing Cuba?"

"I'm long retired. Just in town to visit an old friend."

"Who happens to be the leader of the Free World. Tell me, what's the mood at 1600 Pennsylvania Avenue?"

"Here's about all I can tell you so far. The White House Mess makes a mean bowl of oatmeal."

Volkov appeared behind Miss Dickerson and said, "How nice that you two are getting acquainted."

"Well, Maxim, it was not very polite of you to abandon a guest to our fair city," my uninvited guest said. She turned back to me and asked, "Can I come by the White House for an on-camera interview later this afternoon?"

"Oh, I expect to be on my way back to California by then."

"Please, my dear," Volkov said to her. "It is time for Nathan and me to eat and drink and talk of old days and children."

"So nice to meet you, Mr. Michaels," she said. "I look forward to our next conversation."

Volkov had his eyes on her legs as she made her way back to her Norwegian lunch companion. When he looked back at me, his belly began to shake with delight.

"Thank you so much for rescuing me, Maxim," I said. "But then again, it was your full bladder that led to my being ambushed by a reporter."

"You Americans do believe in your freedom of press," he said between gasps. "We are better at handling pesky journalists in Moscow, even ones who are *krasivaya* ...."

"Beautiful?"

"Yes, even beautiful ones like Mrs. Dickerson."

Chapter Nine

"Cigar?" Volkov asked.

We were hanging on the wrought iron bars outside the White House like tourists. Volkov had eaten enough to keep his huge engine fueled – two pork chops, an order of crab cakes, and a quarter of a lemon meringue pie, washed down with almost a full bottle of burgundy. I had little appetite, but had managed to get down a few bites of hamburger and a half glass of the wine to be sociable.

"No thanks. But go ahead."

"Of course, I will go ahead," he said. He reached into a pocket inside his jacket and came out with a cigar. He peeled off its red and gray band that said "Montecristo" in oversized letters.

"How appropriate to be smoking a Cuban product."

Importing them had been banned since February.

"Yes. I say to First Secretary, 'Why should capitalists have monopoly on pleasure? Let us make friends with Castro so proletarians like us can enjoy world's best smoke.'"

The cigar was damn near as long as a school ruler. "That's one big missile," I said.

He slapped me on the back and then left his hand resting on my shoulder. "I have missed Michaels family humor. In Russia there is little funny anymore. My colleagues are so serious. And here? How is your old friend in White House?"

At last, we were getting down to business.

"He's not happy about having a Russian knife pointed at his heart."

He then reached up to his head. Too late. A gust of wind knocked the fedora off Volkov's cantaloupe of a head. He tried to lean down to get it, but his attempt to fold at the waist left his hand a foot away from the hat on the pavement. A pregnant woman in her ninth month would have had a better chance. I reached down and handed it to him.

We were still bent over, our faces inches apart.

"When we get up, please look at man holding on to fence pretending to admire White House." I caught malodorous whiffs of crustacean, citrus, and wine as Volkov spoke.

I stood and he did the same, plopping his hat back onto his head during the ascent. On the way up I threw a quick glance at a man who might as well have been wearing a sign that said "spy." He was wearing a snap-brim hat, dark glasses, and a trench coat.

"What do you expect, Maxim? Of course, they're keeping an eye on you," I said.

"Or you," he retorted. Our faces were still close enough that I almost gagged at the reek of his lunch. I took a step back, and he put a mitt on my shoulder.

"Who would be following me?"

"Just be careful, my friend." Then he was back to the matter at hand. "You Americans occupy Germany and Korea and Japan, keeping capitalists in power even though they are closer to Soviet Union than United States. So when Cuban workers ask for protection, Soviet Union must protect even though Cuba is closer to United States."

"You need two dozen medium-range nuclear missiles to protect the Cuban proletariat?" I asked.

Volkov's fingers closed on my shoulder for an instant before relaxing. Either he hadn't been told how many medium-range missiles his country had in Cuba or he hadn't expected the American government to know.

"In 1961 the American government tried counter-revolution at Bay of Pigs. A feeble failure. Now your military prepares to overthrow revolution itself. This we cannot allow. Socialism cannot move backward." He stuck a finger the size of a roll of quarters against my chest for emphasis.

"The president is commander-in-chief and will not allow our military to invade Cuba if you Soviets pull back the knife," I said.

"The First Secretary thinks your president is one with knife, a wooden knife."

"A wooden knife?"

"There is old Ukrainian saying – when one goes bear hunting for first time, one takes wooden knife." As Volkov chortled, a series of miniature tidal waves rippled across his belly.

"I'm not sure I get it, Maxim."

He reached into his pocket and pulled out a gunmetal gray lighter. He turned his back to me to protect the flame from the wind. When he turned around, his cheeks were dimpling and relaxing like the guppies in the aquarium in my boys' room back home. The fish didn't suck on cigars though. "Maybe I did not translate well," Volkov said. "The wooden knife is to clean his trousers."

My mind flashed to the first time I'd flown a Wellington on a bombing run in 1941. Before takeoff, the RAF group captain had told me to keep a tight asshole. I hadn't known what he was talking about until the first ack-ack shells started bursting thirty yards away. The other first-timer on the plane, a nineteen-year-old gunner from Newcastle, had indeed soiled his flight suit. Squatting in his own filth, he'd shot down a Messerschmitt over Lille.

I grabbed Volkov's wrist. "Maxim, the President is not about to shit in his pants. *I* am, but he is not. He's not bluffing. He's ready to go to war if the knife, the steel one pressing against his ribs, is not put back in its sheath. He will not back down unless your missiles in Cuba are removed."

"And if are removed?"

"Then there would be no reason for an invasion." I shrugged. "And my underwear would stay clean."

Chapter Ten

After giving Maxim the first hug I'd given a man since I was a kid, I took a look back. Mr. Trench Coat was gone.

It was fifty paces over to the White House gate.

I'd never seen this guard before, but he still greeted me by name. "Mr. Michaels. Mrs. Lincoln asked to see you."

I walked up the drive to the side door. Now that I'd completed my mission, I could fly home. I just needed to report in.

My sense of direction without benefit of cockpit instruments was so-so at best. Driving to Yosemite or Lake Tahoe or Mount Shasta for a family vacation, I relied on the navigational skills of the copilot, my wife. Here in the White House, with no navigator, compass, map, or unspooled thread to show me the way, I got lost in the labyrinth. I expected to find someone to ask, but the office doors were closed and no one was in any of the hallways.

Finally, I heard voices and came to a room whose open double doors offered an invitation to enter. I took a step into a formal chamber whose walls were covered in shimmering green silk. A jumble of French antique chairs, settees, and tables had been moved over to the right side of the room. Beneath a spaghetti mound of cables, I could make out an American eagle woven into the room's emerald carpet. Under blazing lights, two men on trolleys peered through the eyepieces of cameras emblazoned with the NBC peacock. In the far corner, the network's White House correspondent, Sander

Vanocur, and a colleague were in the midst of a spirited conversation punctuated by dramatic hand gestures. Another half dozen men and women with clipboards were scurrying around as were technicians holding meters for light and sound. In the eye of the hurricane, paying no attention to the storm that swirled around her, sat Jackie Kennedy, hands folded on lap, legs crossed at ankles, eyes on camera, while she talked out of the side of her mouth to another woman who was laughing in response.

A technician came out of the room. He pulled a pair of headphones big as earmuffs down to his neck. "Hey bud, can you tell me where I can find somewhere to take a piss in this place?"

I had passed a bathroom during my wanderings. "Down the hall," I told him and then pointed at the two women. "Hey, what's going on in there?"

"The First Lady is being interviewed about the new National Cultural Center."

Right, just the thing to do with the world on the verge of exploding, I thought. What I said aloud was, "Thanks."

"Thanks to you, bud. I'd've hated to stain the Green Room's carpet."

Well, that name made sense. I looked back in and stared at America's Queen. She didn't look like Kennedy's type from what I'd seen before the War. He'd favored blondes; this woman was dark with two black eyebrows slashing over her eyes. He liked curves; she was lean and on the flat-chested side. He was attracted to vitality; she was the picture of refinement and class. Maybe her appeal was the challenge of conquering – even besmirching – that refinement and class. Or maybe it was a need for a suitable political partner. Then with no warning, Kennedy's wife swung her head away from her companion on the couch and caught me *in flagrante delicto* – I was staring at her and she knew it. She dipped her head and wiggled her fingers at me. Even if a curious match for her husband, she had a powerful allure. I smiled back, and she went back to her conversation. I cast my eyes downward. Did she know who I was? How could she?

I started down the hallway in another attempt to master the White House maze. This time, with nary a wrong turn, I made my way to the office of Kennedy's secretary. Too bad there was no one there to congratulate me on my newly discovered path-finding acumen.

I stuck my head around the corner where typewriters were clacking.

"Ah, Miss Collins."

She started and her palm hit her keyboard. Mistakes had to have been made. A red wave began to rise up her neck.

"Oh, Mr. Michaels."

"I'm sorry. I didn't mean to startle you."

"Mrs. Lincoln said you should go right into the Oval Office."

"You sure?" She gave me half a dozen short, fast nods. "Thank you."

I crossed back through Mrs. Lincoln's office, no more than a vestibule really, and rapped on the door. No answer. I knocked again and then swung the door open.

Kennedy looked up from his desk across the room and gestured me in. He had a handset up to his ear. I looked around. He was alone.

"We will know tomorrow night," he was saying into the phone, "whether Khrushchev will accept the Secretary General's proposal to cease all shipping going to Cuba during the period of these talks, number one. Number two, if he doesn't, we'll know what his reaction will be to our searching of a vessel."

Kennedy listened to the response. Then he said, "Good night, prime minister," hung up the phone, and looked up at me. "Sit down, sit down," he said and motioned me into a wooden chair emblazoned with the presidential seal. "That was Harold Macmillan," he said.

"So I gathered." I read the papers. I knew who the British prime minister was.

As if reading my thoughts and trying to one-up me, he asked, "Did you know his nephew, Billy Hartington, was my sister Kick's husband?"

"No, I didn't know." I did know they were both dead. Hartington, son of an English duke, had been killed in the War and Kennedy's sister Kick in a plane crash a few years afterwards. A lot of tragedy to endure.

"There you go, an Anglo-American alliance, diplomacy sealed by marriage. Pretty nineteenth century, wouldn't you say? Anyway, tell me about the meeting with your family friend."

I did.

"Good work," Kennedy said when I'd finished five minutes later.

"I'm all done here, then?" I asked, unsure what I wanted his answer to be.

"Not quite yet. We need to give Khrushchev a way out, an excuse for withdrawing the missiles. He doesn't want to start a war. It would interfere with the unstoppable march to the workers' state. I figure he has Volkov here in Washington because he's KGB and not a diplomat. You're not either."

"So the Russians can deny the whole thing if it doesn't work out," I said.

"So can I." He grinned. "If the CIA did know what you were up to, I don't think they'd be tickled. You're an amateur."

"I am. Perhaps I should go home."

"You know, my father was ambassador in London. Back in March 1939 this amateur, a reporter – Ian Colvin was his name – told the British prime minister and foreign secretary he had information from a top-notch source that the Germans were about to invade Poland. So what did the Brits do? They issued a statement guaranteeing the borders of Poland."

"You're saying without this newspaper reporter the Germans might have invaded Poland without the British declaring war?"

"I'm saying you don't have to be secretary of state to have a role to play in a crisis." Kennedy shrugged. "Here's what you need to do next. Tell your buddy Maxim that we've spoken. Tell him again, very unofficially, that if the missiles and bombers are withdrawn, you'd bet you can convince me to promise not to invade."

"Really? My hint along those lines didn't seem to have much impact."

"Tell him again. Tell him you'll get me to promise publicly." He hit his right fist into his left palm. "Are you up for this cloak and dagger stuff? It can't be as bad as a bomber run over Germany."

Each time I took off during the War I expected to die, at no time more than at three thirty on the morning of October 14, 1943. The moment I entered the briefing room and saw the red yarn on the oversized map stretching from our base in southeastern England to Schweinfurt in Germany, I figured this was it, the end. Twelve B-17 Forts from my squadron took off with hundreds of others heading for German ball-bearing factories. Now in the movies a plane hit by flak would corkscrew downward, black smoke and shrill whine signaling its fate. On this mission, the first condemned plane from our squadron tumbled end over end, making no noise audible over the pulsating screech of our own plane's Wright Cyclone engines. The second took a direct hit and exploded into a flaming red chrysanthemum. Our own Fort lost pressure in the number one engine as we approached Schweinfurt and, later, we had to feather another when it caught fire over the Channel. Our airspeed indicator froze and we stalled twice. Still, the bombardier said he'd dropped our payload of ten big, ugly, blunt-nosed 500s right on the target.

In the end only our plane and two others from the squadron made it back to base. After landing, on my way to the hatch, I skidded on the frozen blood, vomit, and urine that covered the floor. I took off my oxygen mask, dumped out the drool, and counted twenty-seven holes in our fuselage, most marble-sized, one large enough to stick my head through. Three wounded, the radio man critically – his right hand had been shot off – but all ten of us were alive.

I knew Lady Luck wouldn't stick with me. At the previous morning's briefing in the big, half-cylindrical Nissen hut, I'd sat next to those whose bunks were now empty and then eaten sunny-side-up eggs with them in the mess. I saved a seat for one pal before I remembered. At mail call I flinched at the letters from sweethearts and wives back home that had come a day too late. What I had at home – well, it didn't matter. My case for mercy was weak.

So I resigned myself to dying and with that resignation came regret – regret that I wouldn't grow old, see my parents and sister again, get married, have a family, read the newest John O'Hara, see Cal beat Stanford in another Big Game.

Now I felt something more gut-wrenching than regret. I was scared, scared of being counted on and not delivering, scared of my wife and kids dying because of something I did or – more likely – didn't do.

"It's worse than the flying for me," I said to Kennedy. "More waiting. More at stake."

"I know what you mean," he said. "This is worse for me than the run where I got my PT boat sliced in half."

So he was scared too. Courage was doing the right thing even when it was hard. Despite myself, I had to admire the guy. He stared at me and then jerked his head up and down two times.

"I knew it," he said. "You *will* do. Listen, the ExComm is meeting in the Cabinet Room. As long as you're going to be hanging around, I want you to come along."

"Why?"

"I need someone in there who can be dispassionate, who isn't running a government department."

"Why?" I asked again.

"Two reasons. You don't like me much." He waited a beat in case of a protest, but I don't think he really expected one. "You won't be toadying up to me. I need to get perspective from someone like that."

"And reason two?"

"You don't have a job in the government. I always say it doesn't matter where you stand, it matters where you sit. So of course, LeMay wants to unleash his bombers and missiles. He's head of the air force. If he was secretary of state, he'd want to parley."

LeMay was a warrior by nature, but I saw what he meant. Your job determines your position on an issue more than your ideology.

"What about your brother?" I asked.

"He *is* my brother first. But next he's Attorney General. He's a player, not a dispassionate observer."

Mrs. Lincoln stuck her head through the doorway and trilled, "They're ready for the ExComm meeting."

It took Kennedy a few seconds to straighten up. Then he held his hand up like a platoon sergeant and dropped it. I was to follow.

A minute later, the president slid into his chair at the head of the cabinet table. I sat behind him against the wall. A quick look around the room and I could see what Kennedy had been talking about. Three different teams were competing. The first, the Washington Diplomats, was managed by Secretary of State Dean Rusk. Ex-Ford Whiz Kid and current Defense Secretary Robert McNamara along with Chairman of the Joint Chiefs Maxwell Taylor commanded the Pentagon Warriors. The roster of the home team, the Palace Guard, included presidential counselor Ted Sorensen, reputedly the main author of Kennedy's Pulitzer Prize-winning *Profiles in Courage*, the egghead McGeorge Bundy, Wall Street multimillionaire and Treasury Secretary Douglas Dillon, and the president's own brother.

McNamara was saying, "I think to start with a passenger ship, sir, I think there are big problems."

The cagey Soviets were going to challenge the quarantine with an East German passenger ship. The intelligence was indefinite but the guess was that it was carrying over 500 Czech technicians to Cuba. "If we were to force it to halt and damaged the ship, with all those passengers on board, and then find out it does not include items on the prohibited list, haven't we weakened our position?" McNamara asked.

Sorensen thought not. "The East German ship came up, so we stopped it. At the same time, we did not engage the prestige of the Soviets."

After half an hour, Kennedy ended the discussion. He didn't want to chance sinking the ship while an appeal from the United Nations Secretary General was pending. "We'll let this one go," he said.

Like the Tin Woodman in need of oil, he creaked himself upright and headed out of the room. He looked over at Sorensen, then his brother, then me.

We followed like sheep after a bellwether. Back in the Oval Office, Kennedy eased himself into his rocking chair, Bobby plopped in the closest armchair, and Sorensen and I took the two ends of the couch.

Mrs. Lincoln ducked in too. From the doorway she called out, "The Security Council session is on now, Mr. President."

"Turn on the TV then, please, Mrs. Lincoln."

"I hope Adlai shows some guts," said Bobby.

"Can't blame him if he doesn't," the president said. "Not after what happened to him last year."

Sorensen turned away from the president toward me. "Stevenson showed the Security Council a photo that was supposed to be a Cuban Air Force plane that had bombed Havana. The papers found out it was a CIA mock-up. Even the bullet holes were made by company men shooting their 45s into the fuselage." He pointed to the screen, which had finally warmed up. "That's Valerian Zorin, the Soviet ambassador, in the chair."

In the middle of the Security Council Chamber stood a table where its fifteen members sat, but a standing crowd of diplomats and onlookers encircled them. On a wall behind the members spread a huge tapestry of a phoenix being reborn amidst ashes. The symbolism was not subtle: this was the world emerging triumphant from World War II. But a phoenix lived a thousand years, not seventeen.

Stevenson, four chairs away from the Soviet chairman, pushed aside his notes. "Do you, Ambassador Zorin, deny that the USSR has placed or is placing medium- and intermediate-range missiles and missile sites in Cuba?"

Zorin's reply came through the translator. "I am not in an American courtroom."

"You are in the courtroom of world opinion right now," came Stevenson's riposte.

"You will receive your answer in due course," the Russian said. "Do not worry."

"I am prepared to wait for my answer until hell freezes over, if that is your decision."

Kennedy's right fist thumped into his left. "Terrific. I never knew Adlai had it in him. Too bad he didn't show some of this steam in the '56 campaign."

Bobby and Sorensen laughed. The president and I kept our eyes on the screen. The camera turned its eye toward Stevenson's aides, who were putting up easels to hold oversized reconnaissance photos of the Soviet missile sites.

"I only wish *those* photos were fakes," Kennedy said.

Chapter Eleven

"Wait, wait." Bobby held his hand up. When he had our attention, he pointed back up to the TV.

The chic Mrs. Dickerson, her red suit a less flamboyant gray on the black and white telecast, stood in front of the White House, not far from where Volkov and I had been a couple of hours ago.

A decades-old photo of me in uniform flashed on the screen.

Oh, shit. I covered my face.

"In a further confirmation of the increasing chances of hostilities," she was saying, "CBS News has learned that President Kennedy has summoned trusted advisor Nathan Michaels to the White House for consultations on next steps regarding the Soviet missiles in Cuba. At dawn yesterday morning, Michaels was flown by government jet from California where he works for defense contractor Hewlett-Packard Corporation. In an exclusive interview, Michaels, a retired Air Force lieutenant colonel and expert on bombing tactics, confirmed he had been meeting with the President. This is Nancy Dickerson, CBS News, at the White House."

"That's enough," Kennedy said. Sorensen went over to the TV and twisted the power off. "Nate, Nate. I didn't figure you for a glory hound. You going to take a run at Kuchel's senate seat?"

"She was at the restaurant when I met with Volkov. She ambushed me when he went to the men's room. I didn't ...."

Kennedy waved me to stop and began to laugh. With each guffaw his rocker moved faster. The outrage on Bobby's face melted into a toothy smile. The sternness fell away from Sorensen's face too.

Just a moment before I would have suspected the leader of the Free World of having fallen prey to battle fatigue, the rocker slowed and the guffaws slid into chuckles.

"Your face, Nate," he said between breaths. "I wish you could have seen it. Welcome to Wonderland on the Potomac."

That evening was a replay of the previous one. I called home, said good night to my wife and kids, put on my pajamas, and turned off all the lights except for the one on the nightstand. I picked up *Seven Days in May*. After half an hour of literary futility, there came a knock. I knew who it was, and he was coming in no matter what I said. I remained silent.

Kennedy didn't wait more than two seconds before opening the door. He flicked the overhead light switch and strode in.

"I need to use the bathroom," he said. "Okay with you?"

Still blinking from the lights, I said, "It's your house." I looked down at my watch – quarter past twelve.

He left the bathroom door open. "I want to talk to you about the ExComm meeting," he called over the noise of his stream.

When he came out, he was wiping his hands on a towel. "You know, taking a piss is the one thing I do nowadays where I know I'll feel better after I'm done than when I started." He smiled.

What else could I do? I couldn't help it this time. I laughed. "Is it the job or your age?"

He tossed the towel back through the bathroom door on to the tile floor. He grabbed a chair from under the window and straddled it, his chin resting on its back. Only then, his eyes fixed on mine, did he answer my query. "Both. The accommodations okay?"

I looked at the rose wallpaper featuring George Washington, the mirrors framed in polished mahogany, and then back at the sleigh bed where I roosted. "A step above Howard Johnson's and thus out of my league."

"That's Jackie's doing." He shrugged. "What can you do? They call this the Empire Guest Room. I think the bed you're sitting on is on loan from the Smithsonian."

"Empire? *Way* out of my league then. You should have saved it for Hirohito."

"Okay, if he rings the doorbell, we'll say *sayonara* to you. Although, come to think about it, you're moving up the VIP list here in town. NBC and ABC are accusing the press office of favoring CBS. They want to interview you too. McNamara says General LeMay wants to know what a B-17 squadron leader knows about missiles and B-52s."

"I didn't ...."

"Don't worry about it. I didn't come up here to talk about your newfound fame, but I do want to know your impressions of the Ex-Comm this afternoon."

I realized my right hand was rubbing against the side of my face only because of the sandpapery feel of my late-night stubble. I dropped the hand.

"Some of your staff have itchy trigger fingers," I said.

"During the War, the guys back in Washington would pat themselves on the back if casualties were in the hundreds and not the thousands. Well, my crew on the PT boat saw it differently. They weren't ready to die even if the admirals in the Pentagon were ready to chalk up their deaths as a cost of war. They weren't looking to be heroes. They just wanted to survive. A B-17 crew would be the same?"

I thought about the copilot in my first Fort. He was at least as good a flyer as I was, but all he lived for was to get out of the war. The navigator was best in the squadron, but he didn't give a damn about becoming a lead. He just wanted to get back home and chase skirts at Ohio State again.

I nodded.

Kennedy nodded back. "People want to live. I'm not sure the guys downstairs get that."

"They figure a few million casualties in exchange for an end to the Soviet threat is a good deal?"

"Listen, I'm no appeaser. I told you I won't leave those bombers and missiles in Cuba and I'm willing to blow them up and send the whole island to Kingdom Come. But I want to make sure we can't get them out with words first."

Chapter Twelve

I must have incorporated the ringing phone into my dream for a while, but eventually it crashed through the Berlin Wall that separated sleep and consciousness in my brain.

"Hello."

"Hello, Mr. Michaels. This is the White House operator. I have a Miss Leontieva on the phone for you."

"What time is it?"

"5 A.M., sir."

"Who wants to talk to me again?"

"Natalya Leontieva."

"Never heard of her."

"She says she is calling on behalf of Maxim Volkov."

"Okay, put her through."

"Hello?" I said.

"Mr. Michaels, this is Natalya Leontieva. We met yesterday at the embassy."

I recognized the Garboesque voice of the receptionist with the hair-helmet.

"Yes."

"Comrade Volkov needs to see you now."

So he'd heard from Moscow already. Had Khrushchev agreed to pull the missiles out in return for a promise not to invade?

"Where?"

"At the embassy."

"Okay, tell him I'll be there in less than half an hour."

On a list of Volkov's virtues – his gusto, gift for friendship, delight in good food – personal hygiene would not be found. Well, when in Rome....So I didn't bother showering. I pulled on the same clothes I'd worn the day before. On the way to the side door of the White House, I passed a Secret Service agent, but the guard at the gate stopped me.

"Where are you going, sir?"

"A meeting."

"It's 5:15. I'm not sure how safe the streets are. Do you want to be out walking now?"

"Want to? No, I don't."

"What if I'm asked where you've gone?"

"Tell them to ...." Wait. I didn't want this poor sucker to get in trouble. He was just doing his job. Of course, he'd want to cover his ass. There'd been a nice leather-encased memo pad on the desk in my room with a White House logo stamped on the cover. I'd brought it along to take notes on my conversation with Volkov. I scribbled a few words on a piece of paper, ripped it off the pad, folded it in half, wrote "JFK" on its cover, and handed it over. I shoved the pad back into my shirt pocket. "This explains what I'm up to. What's your name?"

"Edward Lane, sir. Thank you, sir. Do you want the president to get it?"

"I expect to be back before he's awake, Agent Lane."

"Good luck, sir."

I wondered if he would read what I'd written. It didn't matter. What would the Secret Service agent make of a note saying I was going to see "our friend V" on Sixteenth Street?

Pennsylvania Avenue might as well have been a country lane. Dawn and the start of rush hour were still a couple of hours away. No traffic as I jaywalked over to Lafayette Square. As I plunged in, the trees hid more of the White House lights. If a mugger were lying in wait, I'd never see him. But even a mugger would need his sleep and there were no odds in working overtime on the off chance that a crazy Californian would scurry by at 5:20 in the morning.

Someone was up early, though, and I had to wait for a Rambler station wagon to whiz by on H Street before crossing and picking up Sixteenth. What did Volkov have for me? *Sure, Nate, Nikita's ready to call off a nuclear exchange if you say so. Let's smoke a cigar to celebrate world peace.* I laughed aloud. The idea that I could hop on an Air Force plane, fly across the country, and pull the world back from the brink of annihilation in little more than a day was a joke – and not a very funny one.

A block from the embassy, the *splat-splat* of a heavy pair of shoes on the sidewalk brought me out of my reverie. I turned around and saw a shadowy figure a couple hundred yards behind me, but no need to worry. If I motored, I'd reach the embassy way before whoever it was caught up. I picked up the pace.

"Michaels!" The voice did not come from behind me, but to my right. I turned and looked across Sixteenth. I was a hundred yards from the Embassy.

"What?"

The reply was a flash, a bang, and a searing pinch on my right ear. What the hell? With one hand on its way to my head, I felt a thump against my chest as if a giant's hand had given me a shove. I flailed a moment and fell back on my ass. Another bang, a mosquito buzz over my head. In the sulfurous light of a street lamp, I saw a man leave the sidewalk on the other side of the street and cross Sixteenth toward me. His gun was drawn. I had a flash of déjà vu back to 1941 when I was flying for the RAF. Over the Channel, on the way back from Holland, a Messerschmitt Bf 109 had locked on to us. Its tracers had shattered the cockpit window, killed my copilot, and sprayed my left leg with shrapnel. I'd figured it was the end. Then as the German fighter moved in for the kill, a Spitfire had come out of the sun above and shot it down.

Here I was again. Maybe two seconds had passed since the last discharge. Now this assailant would finish me off with a point-blank head shot in the time it took him to walk fifty feet. He wasn't wasting bullets till then. I could wait till he got to me or I could run and give him a back in motion to shoot instead of a stationary skull. A slim chance but no real choice. I rolled and put my hands on the sidewalk. As I tried to explode like a sprinter from the blocks, a piece of chewing gum tugged on my left palm. The rubbery tendrils of chicle broke and I took that first step. Then came another shot and a ping as the bullet ricocheted off the pavement.

I'd taken a third stride when an entire fusillade erupted. No bullets hitting the sidewalks or buildings this time, though. I heard a loud "ugh" from across the street and turned. The second round of shots hadn't been intended for me at all but for the shooter who'd been coming to finish me off. Fate had been turned topsy-turvy. He was the one doing the herky-jerky dance of death, not me. It ended with him a collapsed heap on the yellow median line of Sixteenth Street. One last spasm, then stillness. Saved. Again.

Then I heard that *splat-splat* of shoes on the sidewalk again, heading away from me. I turned my head and in the murky yellow light of the street lamps saw the back of a man clad in trench coat and fedora. I wondered if he wore his dark glasses at night.

Chapter Thirteen

"I don't need to be here. I'm fine."

The doc's right hand was moving in and out like a seamstress's, only his needle was piercing flesh, not cloth. It took five stitches to close the flaps of skin where the bottom eighth inch of my ear had been till forty minutes ago.

I'd made it back to the White House gate pinching my lobe to cut down on the blood flow. Lane had radioed for an ambulance and ridden with me. Now here I was with him in a curtained-off space in the emergency room at George Washington Hospital a few blocks from the White House.

"Almost done," the doctor said. "One more stitch."

"How old are you?" I asked.

"I have a baby face. I'm twenty-eight. Don't worry. I know what I'm doing."

"I'm not worrying about you. It's me who doesn't know what the hell he's doing."

"Sir." Lane leapt to his feet and saluted. The doctor hesitated with the needle in my ear, but then pulled it back out. The president of the United States walking into his makeshift surgery was not going to faze him.

"So Nate, what trouble have you stirred up now?" He waved the note I'd given Lane as I left the White House.

"I guess Sixteenth Street here in our nation's capital can be a little more dangerous than University Avenue in Palo Alto."

"You're lucky you didn't decide to walk down the halls of the Capitol," he said. "That's where the real predators lie in wait." He turned to the doctor and read his name tag. "I appreciate your work here, Dr. Lewis. Is he ready to go?"

"He's had a shock, Mr. President."

"I'll bet he saw worse, a lot worse, in the War. Can I take him with me?" Over his white shirt and red tie, Kennedy was wearing a blue windbreaker with the name of the presidential yacht, *The Honey Fitz*, emblazoned in gold letters. He'd shaved too.

"Let me finish checking him over, please." The doctor applied a butterfly bandage to my ear.

I watched beads of half-coagulated blood rolling off my raincoat on to the floor. I wondered if I should write a letter to the manufacturer. Maybe I could make a little spare change endorsing London Fog apparel for use as a butcher's apron.

"Slip off your jacket and shirt, would you, Mr. Michaels?" the good doctor asked, waving his stethoscope. When I tossed my shirt onto a nearby stool, the extra weight of the notepad dragged it to the floor.

"I hope that thing is cold," Kennedy said.

"Oh, sorry," Dr. Lewis said, and blew on the business end of the stethoscope.

"No, I meant it," Kennedy said. The doctor shrugged and stopped his crude attempt to avoid discomforting me. Five inches from my chest his hand stopped moving. "What's this?"

I looked down. What looked like a pinprick an inch above my left nipple was surrounded by a small, rough, dark purple circle. The circle was in turn encased in a rectangle, faint under my chest hair, about six inches high and three wide.

"An unusual place for a tattoo," Kennedy said. He reached down to my shirt on the floor and pulled the notepad from its pocket. A bullet point stuck out about an eighth of an inch from its back. He came over and held the pad against the rectangle on my chest. A perfect fit.

"You are a lucky man," the doctor said.

"Who was the guy who saved me?" I asked.

"I don't know. Who saved you?" Kennedy asked.

"A man in a trench coat shot the guy who was about to kill me."

"Who was he?"

"I don't know," I said. "I saw someone who looked like him hanging around when I met with Volkov this afternoon. No, it's morning now, so I guess it was yesterday afternoon."

"Who was he?" Kennedy asked Lane.

"I don't know, sir."

Then he turned back to me. "The doctor was right. You are goddamned lucky. What if the assassin had used a firearm with decent stopping power rather than a piece of Soviet crap? What if you hadn't had that notebook in your pocket? What if this guardian angel who just happened to be carrying hadn't happened along? Napoleon said he hired only lucky generals. I'm following his philosophy. I want people with good luck on my team. Luck? You got it in spades, Nate."

Lucky, me? True, a couple of breaks had kept me alive. But I didn't want to keep going back to the well. My ration of good fortune must sure as hell be running low by now. It was Kennedy, not me, who – from the first time I met him a lifetime ago – seemed to have a fathomless reservoir of the stuff.

PART TWO

Chapter One
October 24, 1940

I swung the wooden steering wheel around three or four rotations, and my old Ford flivver bumped into the parking lot. After I twisted the ignition key to off, the engine vibrated with a few death rattles before giving up the ghost. I hustled around to the passenger door and swung it open. Miriam extended her right hand. I took it and swept her up and out within a few inches of me. In the flickering light cast by the restaurant's neon sign, I could see the shadowy wave of her lips and leaned toward them. She retreated with widened eyes, lowered chin, and a shake of her head. After I'd straightened up, she came close enough to link her arm through mine, and together we marched through the entrance to L'Omelette.

"*Bonsoir, Monsieur Michaels*," the pencil-mustached *maître d'hôtel* said with a bow.

"Hello, André. This is Miss Coblentz. Just drinks for us." It was already a few minutes after nine.

We were outside the Palo Alto city limits, beyond the mile-and-a-half ring around the Stanford campus where sale of alcohol was forbidden by act of the state legislature. Of course, it wasn't legal even here if you were nineteen like Miriam, but André either guessed her to be older or didn't give a damn. He just played his stock role as Frenchman meeting pretty girl and kissed her hand while murmuring, "*Enchanté, mademoiselle*." After the Gallic pleasantries had been completed, he settled us in a candle-lit corner away from the rowdier-than-usual bar.

Miriam looked up from beneath her eyebrows at me. Sometimes to get away from the law books, I'd lose myself in the dark of the Stanford Theatre in downtown Palo Alto. I had to admire the spunkiness of Vivien Leigh in *Gone with the Wind*, but her appearance did nothing to make my heart beat faster. The Fates had assigned that job to the sophomore opposite who was the little sister of my undergraduate roommate at Cal. This was our fifth date, and I was still trying to cadge a kiss. Not at all like the sorority girls I'd dated last year who seemed to have an agreed-upon timetable that moved from a chaste kiss on the first date to a hand underneath a loosened bra by the fourth, and even less like the more Bohemian coeds I'd known as an undergrad at Berkeley.

"Have you heard from Steve?" I asked.

She made a megaphone by cupping her long fingers around her mouth and called out, "What?"

I swung my head around to examine the source of the din. Amidst the whirling mass under the red-white-and-blue awning that covered the bar area stood a couple of classmates who hoisted beers in my direction. I saw Gordie Hassert's lips form the word "Damn" as someone hit his outstretched arm and splashed a glass of suds over his tweed jacket. Maybe a Thursday night at L'Ommie's wasn't the place for a romantic tête-à-tête. I turned and leaned halfway across the table and tried again. "Heard from your brother?"

She met me halfway and placed her lips next to my ear. "A letter yesterday. He's working on a story about road contracts."

Miriam didn't douse herself in perfume as seemed to be the custom among Stanford coeds. Even in a room hazy with tobacco smoke – she especially hated the stench of cigars – she smelled fresh and clean. I breathed her in.

"Who would have guessed it? Corruption in Nebraska."

When Steve graduated, he'd set out to be a crusading reporter like we saw in the movies. City desk reporter on *The Omaha World-Herald* was the first rung on the ladder leading up to a Pulitzer.

"He likes it there," she said, her breath warm in my ear. She leaned back on her chair and I could see the smile sparked by mention of her older brother.

I held up the menu and pointed to what L'Ommie's called "*vin ordinaire*," fancy French for table wine at six bits a bottle.

She came halfway across the table again and I joined her there. "Just a little for me. A taste. I've never had wine in a restaurant." As she shook her head, her hair swished against my face a first time and then a second.

"Where, then?" I asked.

"Sabbath dinners, Passover."

Steve had wanted me to meet his sister at least partly because I was Jewish too, and there weren't too many Jews at Stanford. The fact I was a red diaper baby raised in a home committed to socialism and atheism — my father was counsel for the longshoremen's union – didn't matter. When Steve and I had gone out to grab a bite between classes, I'd been happy to gnaw on pork ribs while he interrogated the chef to make sure his potatoes weren't fried in lard.

I looked around for a waiter, but the only two I saw were bustling around the bar.

"Let me go put in our order," I said.

She gave me a thumbs-up and leaned back against her chair. She reached into her purse and extracted a book. I could read her lips. "I'll be fine," she was saying.

The diners were done. All the tables were empty save ours. I made it to within a dozen feet of the bar when I came up against the crowd. Half were shouting about Stanford's 4-0 Wow Boys and their football game against Southern Cal on Saturday, the other half about how long England could hold out alone against Nazi Germany. There was nothing for it but to enter the whirlpool.

"Wow! Who's that minxy girl?" Gordie yelled as I nudged him aside.

So I wasn't the only one who appreciated her appearance. I gave what I hoped was a mysterious smile and kept moving with steady strokes toward the bar. Landfall. I put my elbows on the bar and joined the other dozen yelling out orders, but I was the only one asking for wine amidst the shouts for martinis, Tom and Jerrys, and beers. Finally, grasping a carafe, I struck out to reverse my course and swim back to Miriam.

I emerged and held up the fruit of the vine in triumph. But she wasn't looking my way. Instead, she was already sipping wine. Across from her in the chair I thought belonged to me sat a skinny joker with floppy brown hair who downed his glass in two gulps.

"Hello," I said and plopped my carafe on the table next to its half-empty mate.

Miriam smiled and gestured for me to put my head down by hers. She waved toward her new companion and called into my ear, "Nate, I'd like you to meet Jack."

He half stood up and stuck his hand out. "Glad to meet you, fella."

"Nate Michaels," I said.

For someone so weedy, he had a firm grip. I squeezed harder.

"Kennedy," he said. "Jack Kennedy."

Chapter Two

"Did I take your seat?" Kennedy asked.

Pulling a chair over from a neighboring table, I did my best to screw my face into a smile and lie convincingly. "It's fine," I said.

"Jack is a student at the business school," Miriam said.

My swim to the bar had apparently given them enough time to get acquainted.

"Not exactly," Kennedy said with a toothy grin. "I'm just auditing some classes this quarter."

He wasn't telling me anything I didn't know. Young Mr. Kennedy's presence at Stanford had rated notice in *The Palo Alto Times* and *The Stanford Daily*. His *Why England Slept* had hit the bestseller lists last spring. I had turned 23 in May and guessed he was about the same age, but he'd climbed higher on the greasy pole of life. He was an author of some renown and possessor of a self-deprecating charm that appeared to be having an effect on Miriam. I was not happy.

"I would have thought political science was more up your alley than business," I said.

"Why do you say that?"

"I read your book."

"No kidding? I'd heard people bought copies. I didn't know anyone actually read it." He flashed a smile meant to indicate humility.

Miriam swallowed the bait. "Why would people buy it and not read it?" she asked Kennedy.

"Well, I doubt too many people bought it themselves. I suspect my father bought the whole print run and either stashed it in the basement or foisted the books on unwary friends."

Kennedy swung his eyes away from Miriam to me. "What do *you* think, Mr. Michaels? Are we Americans the ones who are asleep now?"

Over his shoulder, I watched a blonde who'd broken away from the pack at the bar heading our way with athletic strides. Tennis player, I guessed. Before I could answer Kennedy's question, she was standing in back of him tousling his hair with her fingers. She nodded at me and glared at Miriam before saying, "Aren't you going to introduce me, Jack?"

He hoisted himself up and flashed an apologetic smile. He introduced Violet Roberts. She gripped my hand with the same surprising strength as Kennedy had. Tennis, almost for sure, with a powerful forehand.

"I am sorry, but we need to go. C'mon Jack. You know the sorority's curfew is ten."

"Nice to meet you, Miss Coblentz," Kennedy said. "I hope we meet again." He took her hand and held it a little too long. Then he grasped mine. "Say, Michaels, tomorrow is Professor Stuart's class on contemporary world politics. You might get a kick out of it. Why don't you drop in and we'll pick up our conversation at lunch afterwards?"

"What time is the class?"

"At eleven in Room 23 in the Northeast Quad."

Why not? I'd've finished trusts and estates by then. "Okay."

I released his paw and he started backing away. "A true pleasure, Miss..."

The blonde Miss Roberts grabbed him around the biceps and twirled him around. She didn't like him talking to Miriam any more than I did.

As they walked toward another couple waiting at the door, Miss Roberts's right arm was coiled around Kennedy's back. Through her stockings I could see her legs were dark except for a pale strip above her shoe tops. Tennis, confirmed.

"From what our guest said, I gather his father has money?" Miriam asked.

The table candles had grown dim. I didn't want to talk about Kennedy, but couldn't avoid the direct question. "His father is Joe Kennedy."

"The ambassador to England?" she asked.

"Right. A real Roosevelt man." I looked down at the table and worked out the upside-down title of her book – *For Whom the Bell Tolls*. "Any good?" I asked in a clumsy attempt to change the course of the conversation.

"Hemingway makes war romantic. He did it in *A Farewell to Arms* and this one even more. It's an argument in favor of intervention in Europe. The hero dies a gallant death fighting the Fascists."

"And that bothers you?"

"I'm not sure .... Hitler is an evil man and must be stopped, but if we enter the war, young men will die ugly deaths. It won't be romantic." She covered my hand with hers. My hand liked the feeling of her cool palm. So did my heart – it was applauding inside my chest.

The crowd at the bar must have taken the departure of Kennedy and Miss Roberts as an example to follow. The noise had ratcheted down enough for us to have a conversation in near normal tones.

"You're worried about me?" I asked.

"And every other boy I know. If they'd take girls, I'd enlist right now." She moved her hand away. "Talk of war gets me riled up. Let's talk about the battles on the football field instead. Do you think Stanford can beat Southern Cal this weekend?"

"It's a little warm in here, don't you think?" Miriam asked.

We were cruising down El Camino Real on the way back to her dorm.

I got the hint. The Ford, though, had its idiosyncrasies. Grasping the window crank on the driver's side door with my left hand, I wiggled it off the shaft. I passed it over to Miriam who reattached it to the shaft on her door and lowered her window. She'd been in the car before and knew the drill.

"Maybe I'll check the junkyard for another crank," I said.

"You don't like sharing the one?" she asked.

"Well, if you don't mind...."

She stuck her face out the window and called out, "The fresh air is the same we'd feel in a Duesenberg."

"Invigorating?" I asked when she pulled her head back inside.

Pushing her hair back, face flushed, she replied, "That's for sure. How about some music?"

"The radio hasn't worked since last week and that was only for a couple of minutes."

Miriam wiggled the crank off the shaft on her side and I put my hand out.

"Wait," she said and rapped the crank against the round black face of the radio in the dash. She held it poised for a follow-up, but facing the threat of renewed violence, the radio yielded. "It's glowing now," she said.

Thirty seconds later we were joined in the front seat by the voice of Sinatra crooning "Fools Rush In" for the Tommy Dorsey Orchestra.

We pulled up in front of Mariposa Hall at 10:28, two minutes before curfew at the dorm. Miriam didn't wait for me to open the car door this time. I followed as she trotted up the concrete pathway. At the entryway, she turned around and handed me the window crank, but I wanted a more memorable goodbye. A female matador avoiding an onrushing bull, she took a step to the side. I missed my target, but my lips did land just under her ear. The way she arched her neck and sighed – she might as well have waved a red cape. Huh. So she acted cool, but was hot-blooded. I reached for her. She sidestepped me again and twisted the doorknob.

"Barely made it, Miss Coblentz," came the house mother's voice. Then came a door slamming in my face and a metallic key rattling in the lock.

Chapter Three

"You were in England last year," I said. "Do you think they can hold out?"

Jack Kennedy and I were in the student union, the muscles in our jaws working hard to grind up the gristly burgers we'd been served.

"Three months ago I would have said no, but the Brits are holding their own."

"What's your father telling the president?" I asked.

"Listen, I don't want to talk about my father. This is my opinion, not his. We'll be at war with Germany inside a year, two at the most."

"Why do you say that?"

"Have you read *Mein Kampf*?" he asked.

"Yeah."

"Well, you know then that Hitler's crazy, and he won't stop on his own. The French are beaten. The Ribbentrop-Molotov Treaty keeps the Russians out of the fight. The Brits are isolated. It's got to be us."

"Lindbergh is trying to keep us out," I said.

"If the Lone Eagle has his way, we'll just skip over the fighting and sue for peace with Germany now. He's an egocentric, isolationist, anti-Semitic ass." He looked at me. "You're a Jew. You must want to fight."

"That's assuming."

"That you're a Jew? I don't think Miss Coblentz would be seeing you if you weren't Jewish too."

He'd gotten pretty far in a few minutes' conversation, hadn't he? "Fair enough, and what about assuming that since I'm a Jew, I must be an interventionist?"

"You're right. It's another assumption and maybe not a good one. I'm an Irish Catholic. People assume I'd be against intervention because Ireland is neutral, and I'd naturally be on the opposite side of the English oppressors. They're wrong."

Kennedy turned his head to watch a girl carrying her tray coming toward us. She tossed her hair without looking at him and sashayed past, knowing his eyes were on her. I chewed and waited until he turned his attention back to our conversation.

"Your assumption about me is not all wrong," I said. "My grandfather left Minsk sixty years ago to get away from the pogroms in Russia. Hitler is even worse for the Jews than the czars were. But I don't think America should fight Hitler *just* because he persecutes Jews. Hitler's no friend of the working man either."

"Ah, Mr. Michaels, you're a Red?"

"No, that's my dad and I don't want to talk about *my* father either. Me, I'm for what's best for the most people."

"Oh, you're a follower of John Stuart Mill? A utilitarian?"

"So Harvard has a philosophy department?" I asked. Kennedy laughed good-naturedly. "For me it comes down to this," I continued. "We Americans should fight now because if we wait, it will be too late. I agree with you. Hitler won't stop on his own. If he beats England, he'll come after us next. And he'll be harder to beat if he can draw on the resources of all Europe."

"So what are you doing in law school if we should be fighting?"

"I'm not sure how long I'll stick around." I took a gulp of a new favorite – Dad's Root Beer. "About eighty of us took flying lessons last summer with the Flying Club."

"Did you get your pilot's license?" Kennedy asked.

"Yeah, I did. Getting ready. I think this war's going to be about air power. What about you? What are you doing here at Stanford anyway?"

"Well, my brother's law school roommate, a fellow named Tom Killefer, was student body president here at Stanford. He made Palo Alto's climate sound pretty good, and I figured what better place to rest up before the storm?" He smiled. "I love Stanford. Barclay's seminar analyzing the presidential election is interesting, and you saw how good Stuart's class is. Tom was right about the great weather – it sure beats Boston and London all to hell – and, after sixteen years at boys' schools, I'm a convert to coeducation."

"Or at least coeds."

"*Touché*. Why law school for you?"

"I grew up hearing at the dinner table that the law was protector of the common man."

"And I grew up hearing that it was every man for himself. But here we are agreeing anyway. Your dad's a lawyer? What kind?"

"He represents Harry Bridges and the longshoremen."

"Your dad is *Solly* Michaels?"

"You heard of him?"

"I read the papers."

"Not exactly an ambassador."

"Isn't he called 'The Tribune of the Working Man'? Sounds better than a mere ambassador."

"Maybe to *The Daily Worker*."

"I'd really like to meet him. Can we arrange it?"

I liked Kennedy; I couldn't help it. Here we sat, a Russian Jew and an Irish Catholic, one a wealthy apostle of social Darwinism, the other a socialist always short of money, both blessed and cursed with famous fathers. Still, both of us were whiling away time in Palo Alto going to classes, kindred spirits waiting for the gathering storm to break.

Chapter Four

Miriam's mouth formed an O. Above the collar of her beaver coat, the vibrating tendons in her neck indicated she was screaming, but I couldn't be sure. It wasn't only because I had my hands over my ears. No one could have picked out a single voice from the 80,000 students and fans in Stanford Stadium on that Saturday afternoon. Or really 80,000 minus one. I was a Bear, a grad of the University of California 40 miles north of here, the sworn enemy of the Indians playing down on the field.

The whistle blew, and the cheers got even louder. It was halftime. Stanford's Wow Boys were holding their own against the brutes from Southern Cal in a 7-7 tie game.

Miriam finally sat down, breath short and color high.

She yelled something and I shook my head. Couldn't hear. She reached down into a sack and pulled out a couple of cheese sandwiches. She raised her eyebrows in inquiry.

After I'd unwrapped the waxed paper and munched down a first bite, the crowd noise subsided a little and Miriam leaned over. "Stanford will win," she said. Then from nowhere came, "I think there's a risk the English will make a separate peace with the Nazis."

Around us students stopped yelling and started sipping from shiny flasks hoisted out of the deep pockets of fur coats.

She'd voiced a fear of my own. France had fallen in June. Goering's Luftwaffe was pounding English cities. Still, I felt compelled to take the opposing view. "Not while Churchill is prime minister," I replied in a voice just a few decibels above normal.

"The MPs threw over Chamberlain for Churchill. If things go much worse, they could get rid of Churchill."

The couple next to us began rehashing the first half between slugs. Not us. We were going to solve the world's problems.

"So we need to help the English," I said.

"We do," she agreed. "What do you think of Shaughnessy?"

She was making me dizzy with her skidding conversational U-turns.

Last season Stanford had won only one game. This fall they'd imported a new coach, Clark Shaughnessy, from the University of Chicago. On offense he had three backs line up in a row behind the quarterback, who himself was behind the center. Using this "T" formation, Stanford had won its first four games and was facing its biggest test against last year's Rose Bowl champs.

"He's a miracle worker."

———⌣———

With three minutes left, Stanford had the ball, but needed to march eighty yards to take the lead.

Twelve plays later, with sixty-four seconds left in the game and twenty-four yards to the goal line, the ball was hiked. Handoff to the halfback, Hugh Gallarneau. Stopped at the line. I turned to Miriam. "Too bad," I said.

She pointed. Seven defenders had formed a mound of red and yellow atop the unfortunate Gallarneau. But he didn't have the ball. Five yards behind the line of scrimmage, alone in the backfield, stood quarterback Frankie Albert, fingers wrapped around the ball's laces, left arm cocked. He let it fly. Freddy Meyer made a flying circus catch to gather it in on the twelve, where he was brought down by a desperate Trojan defender. Stanford was demonstrating that intelligence, speed, shiftiness, and deception were what it took to beat a stronger and larger foe.

Amidst the screaming and thumping of feet against the bleachers, Miriam put her lips against my left ear and suddenly we were back to world affairs. "You have any ideas on how to help the British?"

I had taken those flight lessons last summer, but I didn't want to mention that. One more pilot was not going to turn the tide. "Send them even more ships. Get ready to fight."

We stopped the dialogue to watch Albert hand the ball off to Norm Standlee, who scampered in for the touchdown and then kicked the extra point. The cheers were loud, but restrained. All knew the mighty Trojans could still steal a victory from the Stanford eleven with a score in the game's last minute.

As if she'd heard what I'd been thinking, she said, "Each person has to do whatever he can. Public opinion has to support more aid to England."

"How?" I asked.

"You heard of the White Committee?"

Kansas newspaper editor and publisher William Allen White had started the group last May to lobby for support of England.

"Sure, what about it?"

Whatever she said in response was drowned out by the roar of the crowd as Stanford kicked off. Now Southern Cal had the ball on its twelve. I looked over at Miriam, but her eyes were on Woods, the Trojan tailback. He cocked his arm and threw the pigskin right into the hands of the waiting defender – who else but Frankie Albert? He ran it into the end zone and scored. Thanks to him so did I. In her rapture Miriam turned to me and pushed her lips against mine.

Her mouth opened into a real kiss that lasted until the last of the 80,000 could scream no longer.

When we pulled apart, she was panting. "That was wonderful."

The touchdown or the kiss? No matter. I was ready to betray my alma mater and start rooting for Stanford myself in return for such a reward after an Indian victory.

Chapter Five

"You sure you know what you're doing?" I shouted above the whooshing whine of the wind.

The brand new, red-seated, bottle-green Buick convertible handled just a trifle better than my nine-year-old Ford Model A. Kennedy had his right foot pressed down on the accelerator. A glimpse at the speedo showed we were zipping up the Bayshore at seventy miles per hour.

"A chance to meet Solly Michaels?" Kennedy called back. "I wouldn't miss it."

"And if your father finds out?" Leaning forward over the wheel, he didn't hear me over the rush of the airstream and the growl of the V8. I called out again, "And if your father finds out?"

It was the wrong thing to say. When Kennedy started laughing, his eyes crinkled shut and the front of the car stopped following the road and veered toward San Francisco Bay.

He opened his eyes a second later, in time to twist the wheel to the left and save us from being lost at sea.

"Well, if my father finds out I'm having Sunday lunch ...."

"And skipping church," I added.

"My father wouldn't give a damn about that. Now my mother's a different story. Anyway, if my father found out I was lunching with a bunch of Reds ...."

"Jewish Reds," I added.

"Ah, my favorite kind. You have any idea who's going to be there?"

"My mom and dad. My sister. There's always a guest or two or ten. Maybe an official from the ILA – that's the union – or a politician or a reporter. We'll see."

"Good chance there will be some Irish there, then."

"Yeah, but we'll outnumber you."

"Look. You seen this ad?" Kennedy took a hand off the wheel to point toward the side of the road.

"I'll look. You drive."

I read aloud from a small sign, "A peach looks good with lots of fuzz."

We were racing by the next sign in seconds. "But man's no peach," I reported.

And the last one, "And never was. Burma Shave."

He laughed at the punch line, but kept his narrowed eyes on the road this time. I did catch him bringing a hand off the wheel and feeling his chin. Now I laughed because I was doing the same. The advertising whiz who'd put up the signs knew what he was doing.

Once we pulled off the highway, I started calling out directions to navigate the narrow streets of the Forest Hill neighborhood where my parents lived.

"Do they know I'm coming?" Kennedy asked.

"Take a left here on Montalvo. No, but it doesn't matter. If a platoon of starving soldiers dropped by, Mom's icebox could handle it."

"Going too fast for you?"

"Make a right here," I called out. Kennedy was in a hurry. He just didn't know where he was going.

When we pulled up in front of my parents' on Santa Rita, Kennedy looked down at his wristwatch. "Fifty-seven minutes door-to-door," he said. "Not bad."

Fifteen minutes faster than I'd ever made it in my Ford.

"Nice place," he remarked as we went up the walkway. A neighborhood of twisty, leafy streets flanked by three- and four-bedroom bungalows, Forest Hill wasn't that far from the docks and the International Longshoremen's Association offices. No place could have been more bourgeois, but because Forest Hill was run by a homeowner's association, Dad's conscience was salved. "The commune" he called it.

I opened the door and signaled for Kennedy to follow. We stopped in the archway leading to the dining room.

Sleeves rolled up, tie loosened, mouth full, Dad was half out of his seat and shouting at a fat man who wore a rumpled gray suit and stained tie, along with cordovan wingtips incongruously gleaming with a fresh spit shine.

"We need to do what's best for the workers, Maxim."

Maxim Volkov stuck his fork into a hunk of poached fish on the platter and moved it into his mouth. He chewed for fifteen seconds while Dad glared. Then he looked up and said in a Slavic accent, "Your country is betraying labor and preparing for war." His fork, a miniature steam shovel, dug into the mound of eggs scrambled with salami already on his plate and deposited a heaping forkful into the open pit of his mouth.

"Daddy, couldn't Comrade Volkov be right?" asked my sister Rosa. Despite being dressed in a teenage girl's outfit consisting of a short-sleeved sweater, pleated skirt, and white ankle socks, she was ready to climb the ramparts for the revolution of the proletariat. Dad encouraged her to take part in these political discussions. "It's the workers who fight and die in wars," she finished.

Swinging her head back toward Volkov for the nod of approval that was bound to await her, Rosa stopped when she saw Kennedy and me. "Nate," she screamed and leapt up, overturning a glass of milk on the bagels Mom picked up from Shenson's Deli every Sunday morning. Rosa ran round the table and threw her arms around me as though we'd been apart for a year rather than a week. I saw my mother getting up from her end of the table and felt my sister taking her head off my chest to inspect my companion a little more closely.

I introduced Kennedy to my mother, father, sister, Volkov, Sean O'Herlihy, an ILA official, and Charlie Sterneck, the ILA associate counsel. Like a magician, Kennedy conjured up a bouquet I hadn't even noticed and presented it to my mother. Where had he found flowers on a Sunday morning?

Rosa grabbed my upper arm and peered across my body at Kennedy.

"I don't think you finished your argument, Sweetie," I said to her.

She paid no attention and responded, "Would you like to sit down, Mr. Kennedy?"

No surprise in finding him seated between Rosa and my mother. I was between Dad and Volkov.

"Orange juice, Mr. Kennedy?" my sister asked, hovering over him. Mom was mopping up the spilt milk.

He laughed. "I'm sure I can manage to serve myself. Sorry to intrude. Please feel free to continue the discussion."

"Well, the war in Europe is a capitalist war and I was saying we should stay out," Rosa said, chin jutting.

Volkov turned to Kennedy. "Your father is capitalist, is he not? Still, I understand he shows good sense and recommends America stay out of war."

Such was the rumor – that Kennedy's father didn't think the English could win and was advocating isolationism.

Mom intervened. "You know Mr. Kennedy's father, Maxim?"

"Of course. You hear of Joseph Kennedy, America's ambassador to England?"

"Of course," Mom said, showing no surprise that his son was in her dining room. Rosa's eyes widened, though.

"Maxim, it would be funny if Ambassador Kennedy and you were of one mind on world affairs, wouldn't it?" I turned my gaze to young Kennedy.

"I can't speak for my father," Kennedy said. "But I do believe the Nazis worship power and step on the weak. If we are weak, we will be stepped on."

"The Germans are fighting against decadent regimes like English monarchy," Volkov said. "Not vigorous regimes like Soviet Union. The United States is becoming workers' republic and will have no worries."

"Mr. Volkov ...." Kennedy began.

"Please, not Mister," Volkov interrupted. "Term is relic. Call me Maxim or Comrade."

"Okay, Maxim. You know what my father does for the American government, but what do you do for your country?"

"I am third secretary of consulate here."

"And what do your duties entail?" Kennedy asked before taking a bite off his plate.

"Like everyone in consulate, I help maintain friendship and solidarity between our countries."

"So eating the food we put in front of him constitutes doing business for Maxim," Dad said.

Volkov tilted his head back to laugh, but then gagged on the mixture of fish and meat that filled his mouth. Dad reached over to hit him on the back. When the Russian could talk again, he said, "Hardship duty." Then he laughed some more. "Comrade Kennedy, I work hard. What better to do than drink and eat with good American friends?" He speared a piece of fish and brought it up to his mouth. "Ahh."

Prompted by this sound of bliss, Kennedy turned to my mother. "Mrs. Michaels, I have to say this is the best smoked fish I've ever eaten."

"We get it straight off the Matson liners when they come in from Hawaii."

Low pay and long working hours my father might suffer on behalf of the union. The fish did offer a little consolation.

Kennedy turned to my father. "Excuse me, sir. Would you tell me the real story of the '34 longshoreman's strike? Were you there when the police fired on the strikers?"

Volkov could not resist answering himself. "A glorious moment in history of American workers. A general strike, bosses firing on workers, martyrs Howard Sperry and Nick Counderakis .... It brings back memories of October Revolution. Ah, but you should hear from hero of strike."

Dad leaned back in his chair. I'd heard this story dozens of times.

Chapter Six

As we pulled away from the curb a few hours later, Kennedy said, "Thanks for letting me tag along. Your parents are different from what I expected."

"Less ethnic?"

He grimaced with embarrassment. "Yeah, maybe."

"San Francisco was a sleepy Mexican town till the Gold Rush. Jews arrived here the same time as everyone else. They don't count as newcomers here like they do in Boston."

"They came to pan for gold?"

"Sure, some did, but there was a Bavarian tailor who made pants out of tent canvas and brass rivets and a …."

"Levi Strauss. More money to be made supplying the miners than mining?"

"You got it."

"So in San Francisco if your ancestors came at the time of the Gold Rush, it's like someone in Boston being descended from a passenger on the Mayflower?"

"Sounds about right," I said.

"You're an aristocrat, then?"

"Come on, my dad is a union lawyer."

"And your mother?"

"Her family were shopkeepers."

"What kind of shopkeepers?"

"Women's clothing."

Kennedy narrowed his eyes. "What was her maiden name?"

"Magnin."

"Like the department store?"

"Mary Ann and Isaac Magnin were her great-grandparents."

Kennedy clapped his hands in triumph. "So you are from a family of San Francisco aristocrats. I knew it. My dad married the daughter of the mayor of Boston. Our fathers both married above themselves."

From what I gathered at family functions, my mother's parents had not been too pleased with her choice of mates. Still, I was enough of a radical, a romantic, to say to Kennedy, "They were in love."

As we turned back on to the Bayshore to head back to campus, Kennedy said, "Still, a department store heiress marries a red lawyer?"

"Dad might be a socialist, even a communist, but he's no revolutionary," I said.

"He didn't say so, but I heard he did the real negotiating of the ceasefire in '34."

"He'd rather win through negotiation than violence."

"He's a good man," Kennedy said. "Don't know what he's doing hanging around that Russian spy."

"Maxim a spy? He's been coming around for food and political arguments since the Russians opened their consulate, what, six or seven years ago," I told him.

"So *is* he a spy?"

"I don't know, but there's nothing secret about him as far as I can see. He's had different titles at the consulate but his job seems to be keeping in touch with communists, socialists, unionists, and such up and down the West Coast."

"What does that mean, 'keeping in touch'?"

"Well, until summer last year, he'd tell Dad and the union that America needed to rearm to stop fascism and support workers.

Since the Russians signed their treaty with the Germans, he says we need to make sure America is not drawn into a capitalist war."

"Flexible, isn't he?" Kennedy said. "If the Russians could tell the longshoremen what to do, that might mean no aid for England against the Nazis. Is that what he's up to?"

"Huh," came my noncommittal answer. I'd always treated Mom and Dad's Sunday morning discussions as having as much influence on world affairs as my high school debate club matches did. I was naïve. Kennedy was right to be suspicious.

Chapter Seven

At Cal most of my friends had been Democrats or socialists. Here on the Stanford campus in the fall of 1940 anyone declaring support for Roosevelt ran the risk of being captured, stuffed, and displayed in the section of the university museum devoted to rare and exotic species.

Kennedy was waiting for me Monday morning after I'd finished my midterm exam in contracts and convinced me to come along with him to Professor Barclay's seminar analyzing the imminent presidential election.

As we moseyed through the Quad, he said, "Almost November and the leaves haven't turned color."

"You miss home?"

Kennedy looked at the three coeds walking toward us, books under their arms. Their short-sleeved blouses and mid-calf skirts revealed creamy tan limbs. "Hello, Jack," the brunette in the middle sang out while her girlfriends giggled.

"Hi, Thelma."

After the greeting, the three replied in a language of gestures rather than words – flashing teeth, wriggling shoulders, and flouncing walk – which Kennedy seemed to comprehend just fine. Once their saddle shoes had carried them past us, Jack picked up the thread of our conversation. "Do I miss watching the leaves turn color in Harvard Yard?" He shook his head. "Nope. I think Palo Alto has autumn in Boston beat all to hell." He looked back over his shoulder at the retreating trio.

Five minutes later I sat around a long oval table with Kennedy and nine other students, all male. The tweed-jacketed and silver-maned Professor Barclay, who sat at the table's head, had had no problem with me sitting in. "Eight days until the election," he started and then paused to suck on his pipe. "Tell me who's going to win next Tuesday and why." *Puff, puff.* "Mr. Ransom, can you get us started?"

A lean-faced fellow with gold-rimmed glasses leaned forward. "The country has had eight years of Roosevelt socialism. I think it's ready for a change."

Our eyes moved back to Barclay, who was tamping down the tobacco in his pipe's bowl. "You may be ready for a change, Mr. Ransom, but beyond personal preference, what do you base your conclusion on?"

"Uhh." Ransom rubbed his chin and looked at the chandelier above the table as if formulating an answer. We waited a half minute for Ransom's muse to strike. Whittaker, a student who embodied the colors of Stanford's recent football opponent with his red face and straw yellow hair, raised his hand and asked, "May I try, Professor?"

"Okay with you, Ransom, if Whittaker takes a shot?" Still mute, Ransom nodded.

"I think the country knows now that politicians can't do it, can't get this country back on its feet," Whittaker said. "That's why the Republicans were smart to nominate a businessman like Willkie to face up to Roosevelt. Voters are suspicious too."

"What do you mean, 'suspicious'?" Kennedy asked.

"Well, Roosevelt's working for the Jews. The Jews took over Russia for the Communists, and the voters in this country won't stand for it happening here."

I pushed my chair back and started to stand up, but Kennedy laid a hand on my jacket sleeve while he kept his eyes locked on Whittaker. I sat back down.

"You're better informed than I am, Whittaker," Kennedy said. "What Jews took over Russia?"

"Trotsky, for one."

"Who was exiled in '29 and had a hatchet planted in his head two months ago." Kennedy paused for a response. Whittaker's ruddy complexion had darkened to crimson.

"Why would Roosevelt be working for the Jews?" Kennedy continued in a voice of sweet reasonableness.

"Bernard Baruch tells him what to do, so the Jewish bankers can make money."

"The stock market's lower now than it was in the twenties. Maybe Roosevelt's secret scheme is not to enrich Jewish bankers, but to bankrupt them."

All the students save Whittaker laughed. The professor himself might have been stifling a chuckle with a couple of quick puffs on the pipe.

Whittaker stood and yelled. "The Jews don't like Hitler so they're trying to get Roosevelt into the war against Germany."

"Wait. I thought you said the Jews were supposed to be communists. I spoke to the third secretary of the Russian consulate in San Francisco yesterday. He says America should stay out of the war."

Now Whittaker was leaning across the table. "Don't get clever with me, Kennedy. Everyone knows the Jews control Roosevelt."

"Everyone?" Kennedy asked in his Boston twang. "Perhaps it would be better to rely on polling to determine what most people think rather than conversations at your parents' country club."

Before war could break out in the seminar room, Barclay intervened. "Ah, yes, the polls." *Puff.* "Do we think they will be more accurate this time than they were in 1936 when *The Literary Digest* poll predicted a landslide for Landon?" *Puff.* "What do you think, Mr. Johnson?"

Johnson was two minutes into his disquisition on the advanced techniques used by the pollsters Elmo Roper and George Gallup before Whittaker unclenched his fists and leaned back in his chair.

After class, Kennedy and I filed out behind Ransom and Whittaker. "Damn micks are no better than the kikes," the latter said loud enough to ensure Kennedy would hear.

I started for him, but Kennedy grabbed my sleeve again and said in a volume that matched Whittaker's, "That's quite a compliment, Whittaker. We Irish are as smart as the Jews? Quite a compliment."

Kennedy turned and grinned at me. As angry as that cretin Whittaker had made me, I couldn't help myself. I grinned back.

Chapter Eight

"Isn't that Jack Kennedy's car?" Miriam asked as we huddled under an umbrella and approached the snazzy green Buick.

"Yeah, how did you know?"

"Don't be silly. Everyone on campus knows it's his car."

"Not now." I flashed the keys in my free hand.

"Hmm. You could never have afforded to buy it from him." She snapped her fingers. "I've got it. You won it in a poker game."

"Not likely. My Ford wouldn't start. Must be all the rain. Kennedy left me his keys for the weekend." I swung the passenger door open for her.

After I slid behind the wheel, she asked, "You and young Mr. Kennedy are best friends now?"

"He's a great guy. Not what I expected." I put the key in the ignition.

"What did you expect?"

I took my hand off the key and turned toward her. "Well, his dad's rich. He's from Boston, went to Harvard."

"So you figured he'd be a stuck-up snob?"

I shrugged. "Maybe." The raindrops thrummed a rhythmic tattoo against the car's canvas roof.

"And he doesn't need his car because he's away for the weekend?" The curls around Miriam's head formed a glowing halo lit from behind by a street lamp.

"Right. I dropped him off at the station this morning. He took The Coast Daylight down to L.A."

"L.A.?" she asked.

"He has some friends down there, I guess. His dad used to produce movies."

"Friends down there? You've been spending a lot of time with him up here."

"He's a great guy," I said again.

"Well, he is glamorous. You know, Nate, I don't know if I trust him. He's a little glib. A little too smooth. Too much of a ladies' man."

I'd been leaning closer to her, but now I snapped back. "You just implied I was jumping to an unfair conclusion when I first met him."

"You decided before. I formed my opinion after talking to him."

"After one night's conversation at L'Ommie's? What did he say to you?"

"Let's not argue," she said and leaned toward me and brushed my cheek with her lips.

Before she could slide back toward the passenger door, I grabbed her by the arms and brought her closer. "Let's not," I said and leaned down for a repeat of last Saturday's kiss in the stadium. She turned and I ended up returning what she had given me – a brush on the cheek.

We moved apart, and I turned the key.

"Don't be mad. I want to celebrate. Did you listen to the game on the radio?"

"Nope."

"Well, we beat UCLA 20-14."

"Pretty close."

"Only because the Bruins have a fellow named Jackie Robinson who can run through walls."

"They say he can pass pretty well too," I said.

"Still, we won. Do you think we can win the rest of our games?"

I took a deep breath. Again, it was like she was two people, one worrying about the fate of the world and the other the fate of the Wow Boys. I pulled the car away from the curb. "Don't get your hopes up. Stanford plays Cal in Berkeley at the end of the month. Records don't matter in the Big Game, and we are always tough at home."

We were driving between the two rows of giant date palms standing at rigid attention. The fronds thirty feet above the car roof formed a canopy that protected us from the drizzle. "You and Jack Kennedy are a Jew and an Irishman and you can be best friends, but I guess you and I can't?" Miriam asked.

"An Indian and a Bear? Nope, an unbridgeable gap. The Hatfields and McCoys."

"Let's go celebrate anyway."

As we drove into the tunnel under the train tracks, I asked, "Celebrate our incompatibility?"

"We could celebrate that or just being together on a Saturday night."

"Movie first, then dinner?" I suggested.

"Sounds great. You don't mind if I lower the window?"

Kennedy's car did have *two* operational cranks. When I felt the breeze from Miriam's now-open window, I peeked over to watch her close her eyes and lean out to let the rain pelt her face. A honk from the car behind reminded me to keep my eyes on the road and her to bring her head back into the passenger compartment.

"Ah, bliss," she said and, horn or not, I turned to look again. Her face shone like a saint's in a Renaissance painting.

We parked on University Avenue and, arms linked, strolled through the mist to The Stanford Theatre.

"Perfect," Miriam said, her eyes on the marquee.

The top-billed movie was a Jimmy Cagney vehicle called *City for Conquest*, but she was pointing at the other feature listed on the marquee, *The Quarterback*. We'd be seeing that one first.

"Can't get away from football, can we?" I asked.

"If I were a Cal supporter, I'd want to, too," she said.

After loading up on popcorn and Coke at the snack bar in the lobby, we settled in. I looked around. Easy to forget we were in a small college town while enclosed by walls decorated with the crenellations of a Moorish castle and ceilings festooned with twinkling golden stars. My eyes still aimed skyward, my hand met hers in the big tub of buttery popcorn.

"Whoops," she said.

"I guess that's why they call them movie palaces," I said.

She tilted her head. "Are you a mind reader? I was looking around and that's what I was thinking."

The theater dimmed, and we watched Wayne Morris play twins, one a star football player without too much upstairs and the other an egghead studying to be a professor. Inevitably, both loved the same girl. Miriam enjoyed it because it fed her football mania, and I did too, because once the popcorn was gone, we held hands slippery with a patina of salt and butter and because the intellectual, not the glamour boy, ended up with the girl.

We skipped the Jimmy Cagney movie. By nine thirty we were back at "our" table at L'Ommie's. After the popcorn, neither of us was too hungry. I was about to order the scallops, but then remembered Miriam wouldn't eat shellfish. So we split a fillet of *sole meunière* that cost sixty-five cents. We were washing it down with a half bottle of Riesling that set me back another forty cents when I heard someone behind me say, "I saw his Buick out there. Where's Jack?"

I looked back over my shoulder. Violet Roberts's arms were akimbo and her teeth were gritted.

"Hi, Vi. He's not here. I have his car for the weekend."

She relaxed. "Oh, he said he was going to take care of some business down south, but when I saw the car...."

We invited her to join us, but she went back to the bar where she joined a crowd of her sorority sisters and fraternity types.

"I guess she thought Jack was stepping out on her," Miriam said.

"If he were sneaking around, I doubt he'd pick L'Ommie's for his assignation."

When we said goodnight before the formidable wooden doors of Mariposa, I discovered I'd earned a kiss on the lips even without a football victory for inspiration. Progress.

Chapter Nine

"Sixty bucks a month," Kennedy said.

"A pretty sweet deal. I pay thirty-five to live in the dorm."

It was Sunday night. I'd picked up Kennedy at the train station, and now we sat in his cottage on campus in back of Miss Gertrude Gardiner's house at 624 Mayfield. Or rather, I sat on a kitchen chair looking across the room at him sprawled across his bed, a collection of sheets and blankets covering a piece of plywood. Kennedy had supplied me with a bottle of Rainier Ale. He'd stuck a piece of paper under it when he put it down on the wooden table next to me. His own bottle sat on the floor within reach of where he lay.

"You sleep on that board?" I asked.

"And read on it too. Better for my back." From his supine position, he swung his head around. "The place isn't the Ritz, but I can save a little money."

In truth I would have expected this son of the American Ambassador to the Court of St. James to live in a castle, not a one-room cottage. The only pieces of furniture besides the board on the floor where Kennedy reclined, the chair I perched on, and the table where my bottle reposed, were a floor lamp with a glass shade meant to resemble a giant scallop shell and a second chair with a frayed cane seat.

Kennedy looked at me surveying his dominion and laughed. "You think I'm loaded? Well, I'm not. My dad wants me to help him with his memoirs, so he won't pay for me to hang out in California. I'm existing mainly on the money my mother slips me."

My eyes went out to the Buick in the driveway.

"Oh, yeah, that. Well, that burned up most of the royalties from my book. Worth every penny, though." He took a hit from his bottle and held it up toward me. "Green death," he said and managed to get to his feet. I could almost hear his spine creaking. "You want another?" he asked and ambled toward a door that must lead to the kitchen.

Hoisting my own ale, I saw the faint spoor of typewriter keys on the paper serving as my coaster. Privacy be damned. I ran my eyes over what appeared to be a carbon copy.

Her Majesty the Queen yesterday spoke to me about my son Jack's book. Inasmuch as Her Majesty expressed interest, I am sending along a copy of the English edition for her. Will you be so kind as to hand it to her with my sincere regards? Thank you. With all best wishes, always, ...

Through the round circle of perspiration left by my sweating bottle, I saw the note was addressed to The Right Honorable Sir Alexander Hardinge. I reckoned the signature was missing because the original would have been hand-signed by Kennedy's father, the ambassador.

The icebox door slammed shut.

When Kennedy came back into the room, I picked up the bottle in my left hand and flourished the flimsy sheet with my right. "Your book's suitable for royalty, I see."

He gave a dismissive wave. "Oh, that. Yeah, no author's ever had a better publicity agent than my father." I watched him ease back down on his board. Had he left the paper there knowing I'd see it?

Lying on his primitive bed again, he said, "In your family you're the chosen one. I could see that last weekend."

"The chosen one?"

"The crown prince. The one who will move the family up another couple of rungs. The representative of the new generation who will have opportunities the old generation never had. Where did your dad go to law school?"

"He didn't. He did his first two years of college at Berkeley and then studied for the bar while he worked for a labor lawyer."

"Exactly. Now here you are at Stanford Law with all the *gorim* ..."

"*Goyim*," I said.

"*Gorim* – that's the non-Jews, right?"

He wasn't really mispronouncing the word after all. It just came out of his Boston mouth that way. "Right," I said.

"So now you're going to be a big success. Your dad's hopes and dreams are on your shoulders."

I shrugged those same shoulders. "And you?"

"My brother Joe is the crown prince of Clan Kennedy. He's at Harvard Law. Everyone likes Joe. Dad arranged for him to be a delegate to the Democratic convention in Chicago last summer. In the letters I get from my sister Kick, she refers to him as the future president of the United States and she's only half-kidding."

"Weren't *you* named the most likely to be president in your college class?"

He laughed. "Tom Killefer told you that?" He had, but I just shrugged. "Yeah, that's what the yearbook said, but that's not me. It's Joe. You know, I was in England last year. Over there it's the job of the wife of a king or duke to produce a male heir and a spare. My mom did that and more. I was the first spare and then she produced two more after me. Now you, you're the heir."

Was this son of an East Coast multimillionaire envying me, the son of a San Francisco union lawyer?

"I thought you were headed for law school too," I said.

"Maybe. My dad wants me to. And he's tough to resist. What about your dad? Did he push you toward law school?"

"He doesn't mind that I'm here, but he didn't push," I said.

"He just might be a little more subtle than mine. Your dad is a lawyer who's done about as well as he can in his field. Married well too, from what you told me. Anyway, he expects you to do even better in a bigger field. He has to. It's the American story. Your father's father left Eastern Europe to come here? Left on a boat from …?"

"He walked from Russia to France and then took a ferry to England. He left from Liverpool."

"How about that. My great-grandfather walked to Waterford and took the ferry from *there* to Liverpool. He sailed on a ship – it was called *The Washington Irving* – straight to Boston in 1849."

I raised my bottle and clinked it against his. "Same year my mother's great-grandfather left Frankfurt," I said. "Two forty-niners."

He clinked back and said, "Long lost cousins." We drained our bottles and put them down at the same time with a bang. "Yeah, if Grandfather Patrick had gone on to San Francisco, Clan Kennedy would be California aristocrats instead of Boston micks."

I laughed. "He did okay."

"Maybe," he said.

"And he did beat my father's father to America by thirty-seven years."

"Well, your grandfather wasn't in such a hurry. Russia didn't have a potato famine. Anyway, we both have fathers with roots in the old country. They've done well, but they expect us to push the family forward."

"So what are your responsibilities as the spare?" I asked.

"To stand by and wait and not embarrass the family. Another bottle?"

"No thanks. I've got to cram for a quiz on the rule against perpetuities yet tonight. Thanks for letting me use the car. You know something funny? I drove it over to L'Ommie's Saturday night and Vi saw it. She thought you were in there."

"I'll bet she went bananas." I nodded. "Appreciate the warning. Did she say anything else?"

"No."

"Don't look at me with those disapproving eyes. Listen, Michaels, I'm a 'slam-bam, thank you ma'am' kind of fellow. I like the contest between a man and a woman. The conquest, not what comes after. That's how I am."

Miss Violet Roberts had her man pegged, all right.

"Huh," was my only response.

"That Vi is a real challenge. Lucky for her that she's the prettiest girl at Stanford."

"Maybe."

"Okay, you figure it's your Miss Coblentz and you have a good argument, I'll give you that, but back to Vi. I couldn't marry her anyway. She's not Catholic. My family wouldn't stand for it. Period."

He hit his bottle against the floor and some suds sloshed over his hand and dripped on the wooden planks of the floor. "Listen, Michaels, you need to come with me next time I go to L.A."

"Maybe."

"Next weekend?"

"I've got a lot of studying."

"You heard of Bob Stack?"

"Robert Stack who gave Deanna Durbin her first movie kiss?"

"Yeah, that's the one. Well, he's a friend. I stay at his place. I visit movie studios. Come. You will *not* be sorry."

"Let me see how the studying goes."

"I take that as a yes. I'll let Bob know we'll both be down.

Chapter Ten

"Your dad is back from England?" I asked Kennedy.

"Roosevelt wanted him in Washington."

"To get some help before the election?"

"Maybe, but FDR doesn't need help. He's going to win today."

It was the first Tuesday of November, election day, and Kennedy had walked along with me to the polling place downstairs in the Faculty Club. While I'd been busy exercising my right to vote in a curtained booth, Kennedy had amused himself flirting with the professor's wife who oversaw the polling. He himself was still registered in Massachusetts.

"You mean I wasted my vote on Norman Thomas?" I said, naming the socialist candidate.

He punched me in the arm. "Sure, sure. I figured you for a Browder man."

"Count me as too pragmatic to vote communist. Volkov might think we're about to become a workers' republic ...."

"But not you," Kennedy finished. "You're worried about the returns?" He knew darn well I'd voted for FDR.

He and I walked together down a palm-lined path, his hand patting my back as if I were a skittish horse about to bolt. We were taking a roundabout walk to the Union for lunch.

"Right."

"Don't worry," he repeated. "FDR will win."

"Did you see *The Stanford Daily* poll? Willkie 73 percent, Roosevelt 26."

"I doubt FDR even got into the twenties at Harvard, and he's an alum."

I blinked in the crisp sunshine. There in front of a soaring red-capped sandstone obelisk – the almost-completed Hoover Tower still sheathed in scaffolding – a crowd of a couple of dozen were milling around.

Kennedy saw where I was looking. "Some kind of election day rally?" he guessed. "Let's go take a look." His hand on my back directed me toward the small crowd.

Other students were strolling by the gathering on their way to athletic practice or their dorms. Most undergraduates hadn't reached their twenty-first birthday and couldn't vote.

As we came closer, I could read the placards bouncing up and down. "Stand with the Allies. Stand for freedom."

"When I was in London I used to go down to Speakers' Corner in Hyde Park," Kennedy said. "Who would have guessed Palo Alto would have its own Speakers' Corner?"

Standing on a wooden crate decorated with a label depicting lush red Marianelli cherries, a boy with an acne-pitted face was trying to make himself heard. "I would like to introduce the president of the brand new Stanford chapter of The Committee to Defend America by Aiding the Allies."

Ah, that was the official name of the White Committee that Miriam had mentioned at the football game.

There was a polite, desultory round of applause and then there on the crate, her hair glinting like a golden crown, stood Miriam herself.

I shook Kennedy's arm off my back and turned to face him. "Holy mackerel" was all I said.

He pointed back at Miriam, who was bringing to her lips a red megaphone emblazoned with a white S obviously borrowed from a football cheerleader.

"The United States of America has sided with freedom and against tyranny from the day of its birth. Will we turn our back on freedom now? Will we allow tyranny to achieve the triumph in 1940 it could not in 1776?"

"Why should we fight for the limeys?" a tennis-racket-carrying fellow called out.

"Let her talk," I shouted.

Kennedy's hand moved on to my shoulder. He whispered, "Steady."

"Yes, let them fight for themselves ... *and* for us," Miriam was saying. "The best way we can stay out of the War is to help the English now to resist tyranny."

"And just how do we do that?" the same would-be Don Budge yelled out.

I took a deep breath and then a step toward the heckler.

Kennedy's fingers were squeezing my shoulder. "I'll bet she can take care of herself," he whispered.

Miriam acknowledged her interlocutor and then called out through the megaphone, "England thought the Channel would protect them from what was happening in Europe. It didn't. The Atlantic will not protect us either."

"America first," someone called out.

"Always America first," came Miriam's swift reply. "Here is our choice. Support the English in their fight against tyranny or fight the Nazis ourselves later. How can we let the English die for us without helping at all? Can we sit here and do nothing while they resist an evil regime bent on world domination?"

The tennis player interrupted again. "We sent soldiers to Europe in 1917. What good did that do?"

"I am not saying we should send soldiers now. But can we do nothing while they fight for us? Wouldn't that be immoral? Can't we support the soldiers fighting for freedom with the weapons they need?"

I looked around and saw heads bobbing. Students who had been walking by were now stopping and cocking their heads. The gathering of two dozen had doubled in size in three minutes. She had them. She had won them over, not only with her message but with ardor and presence.

"You can't say we supported freedom in 1776 and that's enough," she continued. "Freedom is a delicate orchid that requires constant tending and attention to thrive. Our fathers supported freedom in 1917. Now it's the turn of a new generation, our generation, to stand up and be counted as opponents of tyranny and friends of freedom. It's our turn."

After five minutes more, a coed with a bow in her hair called out, "What can we do?"

"We need to write letters to the newspapers, to our congressmen, to the White House, to support the English. We must help. We must be on the side of freedom now or fight to save ourselves from tyranny later."

I put my fingers up to my mouth and whistled. I stomped my feet.

Kennedy and I stood back and watched as a couple of dozen students surged up to encircle her.

"A regular La Pasionaria," Kennedy said.

"I hope she's not fighting for a losing cause too," I said. Dolores Ibárruri had roused the anti-fascists during the Spanish Civil War with a series of stirring radio broadcasts, but the Nazi-supported Falangists had won in the end.

"It's not going to be easy. Talking about *The Daily's* polls, only 10 percent of the students support aid for England."

"They haven't heard Miriam yet," I said. "What a girl! Let's go congratulate her."

We waited while listeners shook her hand. I came forward when she stepped down from the crate and looked toward us. "You were sensational," I told her and picked her up and gave her a twirl.

"That's enough," she laughed.

I put her down, and she swayed a little either from adrenaline or dizziness.

I'd underestimated her. Her face and figure had masked what was underneath. She was a passionate girl who cared about a lot more than football.

As we walked away, Kennedy said, "That *is* some girl you got there."

"I've got her? I only wish."

"Well, she's got you, doesn't she?"

He had me pegged. I might have been infatuated before. But now it was more.

"She does now," I said.

Chapter Eleven

If I'd been in the ring with Joe Louis, his gloves couldn't have pounded my ribs from the outside any harder than my heart was pounding them from the inside. Miriam said she had a theme due for English tomorrow morning and needed sleep. She'd been up waiting for election results. Roosevelt had won. It was the day after.

We'd called it an early evening and I'd deposited her on the steps of Mariposa at the civilized hour of 9 P.M. This time when I'd said goodnight, she'd put a hand on the back of my neck when I'd leaned down for a goodnight kiss. It doesn't sound like much, but the way she looked me straight in the eyes as I'd approached, the feel of her long fingers .... I was inflamed by that single kiss more than I'd been by the Berkeley coed I'd gone "all the way" with during my senior year.

I stood looking at the door to the dorm and, after a few seconds, did an about-face and headed back down the dark pathway toward my own room, whistling "Happy Days Are Here Again."

"Hey, stranger, going my way?"

I started. "Hello, Vi. You're out alone this evening?"

"You mean, where's Jack?"

"I'd be glad to walk you home," I told her. "Here, give me your books."

I took them and she linked an arm in my free one.

"Well, I'll answer the question you didn't ask," she said. "I don't know where he is. I never do. But you're his best buddy. Don't you?"

Kennedy and I were best buddies? No sense arguing. I did spend more time with him than with anyone else, even — no fault of mine — than with Miriam.

"Nope," I replied to Vi.

We walked through the gloom under a canopy of oak trees for two minutes before she broke the silence. "You know, I really like Jack. I'm crazy about him. Only one problem — every California girl from Palo Alto to Hollywood is throwing herself at him."

"You're frustrating him."

"I don't have much choice."

"No choice?" I asked.

"No choice," she echoed.

"What does that mean?"

"Okay, listen, you gotta promise not to tell Jack, but I'll explain. I'm from a real hick town, Albuquerque. Here I belong to a good sorority and the girls come from better families than me and they're smarter too. I'm not fooling myself. Men find me attractive, but that's the only card I have to play, and I'm going to use it to find a good husband. And that fellow deserves a virgin. Now if Jack wants to marry me, that's one thing. I'd love to be his queen in real life. But I'm not giving up everything for a guy who might be leaving on the next train for the East Coast and never coming back."

She squeezed closer to me. Her breasts were mashed against my upper arm. "Don't you agree?" she asked.

Kennedy had told me he was never going to marry her.

She let go of my arm and turned to face me. A street light behind her outlined her figure but left her face in shadows. "Well?" She reached a hand across and squeezed my shoulder with her tennis-strengthened grip.

"I do understand," I told her.

She laughed. "Which is not the same thing as saying you agree." She let go. "You came up with an answer that's good enough for me without being disloyal to your friend. You're going to make a great lawyer. Now I'm asking for attorney-client confidentiality." She pulled on my jacket sleeve. "This is my stop."

"Good night, Vi. Good luck with everything." Kennedy had met his match. She sure as hell was not the dumb Dora she pretended to be.

"You're a good friend, Nate. You're a good person. Thanks for listening."

She stood on her toes and pecked my cheek. I watched as she went up the path to the rambling, ivy-covered Pi Beta Phi sorority house.

A good person? That's rich. What role had I just played? Confessor to the coeds. And, thanks to Miriam, I was as celibate as any priest too.

Chapter Twelve

"Oh, Jack, darling."

"Hello, Ida."

Our hostess, hair piled up and neckline plunging down, was giving Kennedy an enthusiastic embrace. I sniffed. Ida wore *Je Reviens*, my mother's perfume, which Dad deemed a bourgeois weakness. Showing geopolitical foresight, Mom had stocked up before the Germans overran France last spring. Maybe Ida had done the same.

"Your book was so exciting," she was saying to Kennedy, who must have been twenty years her junior. "I love smart men."

Exciting? It wasn't exactly a potboiler. I was willing to bet a week's worth of lunches that she'd never read *Why England Slept*.

"Thank you, Ida," Kennedy said and moved her out to arm's length.

Against my better judgment, I'd hopped on the train to L.A. with him early that morning. Now it was a little more than an hour before midnight and we were at our second party of the evening. A few hours before, Bob Stack had taken us to one at his favorite hangout, the Garden of Allah, a complex of pink Moorish buildings on Sunset Boulevard. Along with a dozen others gathered around the pool, I'd gotten a kick out of listening to sometime actor and full-time drinker and wit Robert Benchley tell us how he'd glued turkey feathers to his legs and gone to the office of a doctor he'd marked as a stuffed shirt. According to Benchley, the poor quack kept leafing through his medical books in a vain effort to diagnose the malady.

Kennedy himself had wrangled the invitation for us three to this party in Beverly Hills, at the biggest house I'd ever been in. The woman he'd just disentangled himself from was the mother of a Stanford sorority girl of his acquaintance. Everyone seemed to know Kennedy or know of him, because of his father, because of his book, because of his looks. Within seconds we were surrounded.

"Ida," Kennedy said, "this is a great friend of mine from Stanford, Nate Michaels. His father's a prominent San Francisco attorney."

The way Kennedy said *prominent* made it sound as though Dad counted Southern Pacific and the Crocker Bank among his clients, as though he counted my legacy on the same plane as his own – which in truth he kind of did.

Ida's polite, thin smile widened into one of genuine welcome. "So pleased you could come, Mr. Michaels."

No hug for me, but Ida made introductions and then guided us out of the anteroom and into the party. She gestured to a man wearing a penguin suit. Gin had never been my poison of choice, but I didn't want to be rude, and I took the martini off the tray the man held out toward me.

A hundred feet across the ballroom, I could make out a jazz quartet through the smoky haze of smoldering Chesterfields, Camels, and Lucky Strikes. The brunette vocalist, mustached clarinetist, and hunched-over bassist seemed to be pantomiming in the far corner. The shouted greetings and tinkling glasses of the partygoers made it too loud to hear anything distinct except the occasional wail of a saxophone that must belong to a hidden, fourth band member.

I turned to shout something at Kennedy, but he was gone. No, there he was, thirty feet across the room, heading out some

French doors to the back. Oh, my God. Walking in as he walked out was Lana Turner in a spangled dress that must have been spray-painted on. She didn't look any older than Miriam. Hadn't she just divorced bandleader Artie Shaw? I was even a bigger fan of his than of hers. Nothing like his take on *Stardust*. No matter. Miss Turner's arm was now wrapped around the waist of a good-looking fellow with slicked-back hair who had at least fifteen years on her. Wait. Kennedy leaned and shouted something at them, and she laughed and reached around her escort and squeezed his rear end.

I could handle a passel of longshoremen, hold my own in a head-to-head discussion of precedents with a law professor, or argue dogma with a cell of leftist intellectuals at my parents', but I was way out of my league here. All I could do was open my eyes wide and drop my jaw low. Best to head out the back doors to find some place to skulk until my playboy guide had had enough. Getting across the room was no faster than on a Saturday night at L'Ommie's.

Finally, outside. Tiki torches around the pool made shadows dance. Kennedy was already sitting on a chaise longue talking to a middle-aged man. My God, it was Clark Gable. What would Miriam say when I told her I'd been at a party with Rhett Butler? Kennedy said something to Gable, who glanced at him and then turned to peer down at his drink. After half a minute, Gable raised his head again and spoke a few words. This was not a lively conversation filled with droll repartee. What could the King of Hollywood and the Prince of Harvard have in common, anyway? Kennedy should have stuck to his natural constituency – the women.

Across the lawn I spotted a couple of tall palms. Skirting the pool, I made a trek that ended with me leaning against a trunk and viewing the tableau. From this perspective, it felt as though I were at the Stanford Theatre watching these same people up on the screen. I laughed aloud.

"Hey, Mac," came a man's voice from behind the tree. I peered around the bole. I wasn't quite sure how to put together the disjointed jigsaw of men's and women's clothes and flesh I saw outlined in the dusk, but figuring it all out would only make me a Peeping Tom.

"Sorry," I said to the couple and scooted twenty feet away.

Propped against the overlapping rough tiles of bark on another palm, I sipped my gin and vermouth while watching the latest scenes of a live action movie.

From across the lawn, Bob Stack approached with long strides. He must have spotted me and decided that my isolation required his attention – after all, he was my putative host on this Southern California safari.

"Hiding out?" he asked when within a few feet.

"Just watching the movie," I said, gesturing back toward the house.

He turned around himself and downed his martini in two gulps. He had guarded against running out of liquid refreshment by carrying a back-up glass in his other hand.

"Why's Jack wasting his time?" Stack asked. "Clark's a great guy, but all he really likes to talk about is hunting and camping."

The way the flames of the tiki torches reached skyward reminded me of the cinematic burning of Atlanta. In their light we could see Kennedy still trying in fits and starts to engage Gable. From this distance, the actor didn't seem to give a damn.

"Don't know. Jack likes a challenge."

"He should stick to women. With them he's got a gift. He looks at them and they tumble."

"Not all of them," I said.

"About every one I've seen. He's already bedded half a dozen of the most beautiful women in Hollywood. He does better than any actor, producer, or director. He looks, their ankles go in the air."

Now a platinum blonde followed the path Stack had taken across the lawn. She came right up to him and gave him a juicy smack on the cheek.

"Hey, Bobby, does your mother know you're here?" she asked.

"Carole, I'd like you to meet my friend Nate Michaels."

"Pleased to meet you, Miss Lombard." I was delighted to find that neither my manners nor my voice deserted me when I spoke to the highest paid star in Hollywood.

"I've known this tyke since he was twelve," she told me.

"As you might have gathered, Mom and Miss Lombard are old friends," Stack said.

"But I owe him so much," she said to me. "Did you know he was the national skeet shooting champion of 1935?"

"He's too modest to have mentioned it," I said.

"Not so modest when he's talking to a starlet. Anyway, he taught me to shoot too. Well enough so I could out-shoot a certain well-known Hollywood actor, who didn't like losing much." She threw her head back and let loose a deep-throated guffaw.

"That doesn't seem like a recipe for connubial bliss."

"Connubial bliss?" She stretched out her swan's neck and laughed again. "You're some sort of intellectual, are you?"

Stack put in, "He's down from the law school at Stanford."

"Well, Mr. Michaels, I manage my connubial bliss this way. I let my husband win most of the time. He knows I let him, but he doesn't care as long as he does win."

"He values results over intentions," I said.

"He sure does," Lombard said. "Now back to you. Most of the intellectuals around here are lefties."

"And what makes a lefty?" I asked.

"Someone who, if given the choice, would rather let the Communists rule the world than let the Nazis conquer it."

"I guess that makes me a lefty, then."

A few other couples holding drinks in their hands were form-ing a caravan across the darkness, making for our palm-treed oasis.

"So Red Nate, what's going to happen in Europe?" Carole Lombard asked me.

"My opinion's not worth much, but I don't think the Germans can win."

"You think itsy-bitsy England can win?" she asked.

"Napoleon controlled Europe, but couldn't cross the English Channel. History says if you don't beat England, you can't control Europe. And the English don't have to hold out forever. Just until we come in."

"Mr. Roosevelt says he doesn't want to get in."

"So did Mr. Wilson before the last war."

"Bravo," came a baritone English voice. I recognized C. Aubrey Smith, an actor whose screen roles seemed to run the gamut from crusty old English colonels to crusty old English generals.

The conversation picked up. If we'd talked about film, I would've been sunk. But we discussed the world situation. When someone mentioned Lindbergh's pro-isolationist rallies, I remarked, "The Lone Eagle flew to Paris thirteen years too early," I said. "Now that the Germans have occupied it, he'd get a really enthusiastic welcome."

Every observation I made, every opinion I offered, every joke I told, seemed to engender oohs and ahs and nods and laughs. They must have been a little soused – I sure was. In any case, a team of tray-bearing waiters had formed a conga line running from the bar across the lawn to our oasis.

Amidst the chuckling and giggles, someone clapped me on the shoulder. I turned to see the beaming and patriotic Aubrey Smith. Behind him, I noticed Kennedy and Gable had joined our group of fifteen or twenty.

Carole Lombard said, "Pa, this is Mr. Michaels, who seems to know about everything that goes on in the world."

And then I found myself shaking hands with Clark Gable. My palm and five digits were lost in his huge paw.

I in turn introduced Kennedy to Carole Lombard, Gable's wife of a year.

"Oh, the ambassador's son," she said. She didn't seem too impressed, but then look at who she was married to.

Within minutes, though, two young actresses were standing on either side of Kennedy. They looked like a matched set with pencil-thin brows and peroxide-white hair. They exuded none of the healthy athleticism of Vi Roberts, but he didn't look ready to complain.

At about two in the morning, as I put my hand on the knob of the bathroom, it turned from the inside and I found myself face to face with Kennedy.

"Ah, just who I was looking for," he said.

"Wait a second. I really need to use the facilities," I said.

"I'll wait," he said and swung the door all the way open. When he closed it behind me, we were both inside a space bigger than my dorm room. He leaned against the white porcelain of the sink while I relieved myself. "So Carole Lombard thinks you're a genius in international affairs?"

I pulled up my zipper, turned around, and gave him a shrug.

He continued, "Nate, for Christ's sake, I don't like being outshone like that. The world situation, that's mine."

"Excuse me," I said. He gave me access to the sink and I grabbed a bar of soap. After working up a lather, I looked at his reflection in the mirror. "Things didn't go too well with Mr. Gable?"

"Not like they went with you and Mrs. Gable. Don't you ever outshine me like that again."

I saw his reflection flash a smile, but couldn't tell whether he was joking or not.

Chapter Thirteen

At ten to three in the morning, Stack pulled his convertible up in front of an apartment building that leaned back into the embrace of the Hollywood Hills.

"Where are we?" asked the drop-dead gorgeous blonde splayed across Kennedy's lap in the back seat. I'd just seen her in a movie with Barbara Stanwyck – or was it Bette Davis? – at the Stanford. She'd played the little sister.

"Bob Stack's Hideaway, Whitley Terrace, Los Angeles, California," Stack answered in the voice of a train conductor. "All passengers must disembark."

Another blonde was intertwined with him in the front seat, while a redhead sat between Kennedy and me in the back seat.

With the exaggerated movements of the intoxicated, Stack brought his finger to his mouth to signal us to be quiet. We tiptoed up the stairs and waited while he fumbled with his keys.

"Ta da," he said, as the door swung open on a small sitting room crammed to overflowing with a six-foot couch and an armchair.

The ceiling pushed down on us from less than six feet above the carpeted floor and all three of us men were walking like Lon Chaney in *The Hunchback of Notre Dame*. Then we heard a *thump, thump*, moving across the floor of the apartment below us.

Stack went over to a bottle of Scotch on the mantel and filled a beer stein to within an inch of the rim. When someone knocked on the door, he took the whiskey with him to answer it. There in the hallway stood a man who hadn't shaved in a couple of days and whose right leg from the knee down had been replaced by wood – a modern-day buccaneer. As if to confirm his identity, a piratical "eh-eh-eh" came from his mouth. He grabbed the mug from Stack, spilling a little of the golden elixir, and started thumping back down the hallway.

Once the door had closed, Kennedy asked, "Who was that, Long John Silver?"

The actress with him – what was her name again? Iris, Frances, Lois, something with two syllables ending with an *ess* sound – started laughing so hard that her right breast popped right out of the top of her dress. Her chortles slowed down but didn't stop as she tucked the wayward bosom back into its holder. None of the others paid much mind.

"That's my landlord," Stack said. "He demands a ransom for permitting late night company."

The redhead who'd been assigned to me sat on the couch, hands folded, at the other end of the couch from Stack's blonde.

"Come here, Michaels," Kennedy said. "Let me show you this." He swung open an inside door, and I followed him and his actress into a cramped room filled wall-to-wall by a double bed. Here, the ceiling was so low the blonde had to crouch too. She crawled onto the bed and Kennedy slipped off his shoes and laid down next to her. After she nestled her head in the crook of his arm, she stared upwards at the dozens of flags plastered on the ceiling.

"Let me explain the rules," Kennedy said. He winked at me. "If you can't name the flag, you have to take a drink." He reached to the other side of the bed and came up with a bottle of gin. "Let's start. You pick."

She pointed to a banner of green, white, and red stripes.

"Italy," Kennedy said. "That's right, isn't it, Michaels?"

I nodded.

"Now your turn." Kennedy pointed at a flag.

"The Red Cross?" she guessed.

"Close. It's Switzerland. Here you go." He handed her the bottle and she took a mighty swig and started laughing again.

I closed the door behind me and sat between the two women on the couch. Stack supplied us with tumblers filled with Scotch.

"Where are you girls from?" I asked.

I must have dozed off. A lamp half-lit the sitting room, but I sat alone on the couch. I looked down at my wristwatch. A few minutes after four.

Where had the other five gone?

I stood up. Mistake. I banged my head. "Damn." I scuttled over to the bedroom door and swung it open. Another mistake.

There under the low ceiling, I could see the dim outline of Kennedy lying face up. Astride his hips kneeled the actress whose name I couldn't remember. Her ivory bottom was moving side to side – appropriately enough – like a flag flapping in the breeze. Kennedy turned his head toward the doorway and winked again.

I fell back to the living room.

About ten minutes later, Stack returned. "I brought the girls back home," he told me. "You conked out. Tsk, tsk. Before that, Eve said you were a perfect gentleman."

"Blame my parents."

"She kind of implied you could've screwed her."

"Sorry to let her down. I need to build up stamina for these late nights, I guess."

"You really weren't looking for action, were you?" he asked.

"No, I guess not."

"You gotta girl?"

"Yeah."

"You're a sap."

"Maybe."

"Too bad for you. Did Jack show you our flag game?"

"He did. A lot of flags to know."

"We've memorized them all. We can't lose."

— ‿ —

"Here's your breakfast, gentlemen."

Stack had dropped us off the next morning at the newest wonder of Los Angeles, the one-year-old Union Station. Now we sat with a couple of hundred other travelers breaking their fast at Fred Harvey's restaurant inside the terminal.

The waitress, around seventeen or eighteen, wore an outfit consisting of a white jumper and black blouse. She swung the plate of scrambled eggs and crisp bacon and buttered toast down in front of me. When she did the same for Kennedy, she flashed him a dimpled smile. When he offered a crooked grin in return, a red flush appeared over her high collar until it suffused her entire face. She scurried off with a curtsy, and Kennedy's eyes followed her.

"I wonder if the waitresses' uniforms here were designed by the same guy who came up with a nun's habit," I said.

"Interesting question," Kennedy responded. "They are both black and white, and they both disguise the wearer's charms pretty effectively. Here's the difference though – a Harvey Girl is an angel of God's mercy while a nun is an instrument of God's vengeance." He rubbed his knuckles. "Oh, what Sister Aloysius could do with a ruler. DiMaggio would envy her swing." He looked back at me. "You bring books along for the train?"

"Yeah. My property casebook and *Appointment in Samarra*."

"By John O'Hara, isn't it?"

"Right. Roosevelt might have had a rendezvous with destiny. The character in this book has one with death."

"You've read it before?" he asked. When I nodded, he said, "If you figure it's worth reading twice, maybe I'll give it a try."

The ceilings vaulted sixty feet overhead. Directly above my noggin dangled one of a dozen huge light rings suspended by the lightest of wires. Great. Here I sat in Union Station, breakfasting under the Sword of Damocles. As I kept staring upward, the ring of light transformed itself into the white of an eye and the dark middle became a black pupil. Now I had the eerie feeling of being watched from above. Not enough sleep.

Kennedy had followed my stare. "Look at this place. Garish, overdone, beautiful. I love L.A."

"So I noticed," I said, returning my gaze to him.

"Oh, last night." He waved a hand. "She was willing and I was able."

"I noticed that too. Sorry to intrude."

"No matter. With my back, it's better for me if the girl's on top."

"Glad you're protecting your health."

"You mad at me?"

"What about Vi?"

He tilted his chair back and flashed his teeth. "I'm not leading her on."

Shrugging, I said, "Nope, I guess you're not."

He stuck out his hand and I took it. "You're a great friend," he said as we shook.

Right then the loudspeaker blared, "All aboard The Morning Daylight to Santa Barbara, San Luis Obispo, and San Francisco on Track Eight."

Twenty minutes later we were click-clacking along the rails, leaving behind a weekend that seemed more celluloid dream than life lived.

Chapter Fourteen

The lights in the law library flicked on and off in warning. I looked at my wristwatch. Quarter to ten. Fifteen minutes to closing. I'd had enough jurisprudence and slammed my hornbook shut with a bang. Ever since returning from L.A. three days ago, I'd been restless. Tonight I'd planned to make life more interesting by having dinner at L'Ommie's with Miriam, but she'd left a message at the dorm saying she needed to study for an English mid-term tomorrow. I'd have to wait to see her on Saturday for the football game against Oregon State. Why not call it an early night and catch up on my sleep?

If my law books had been stupefying, the crisp autumn air served as a tonic. When I'd gone into the library at four, the sun had been shining, but now I had to keep moving to stay warm. I strolled down Mayfield Avenue toward my dorm. Then out of the dark, a car came careening around the corner of Santa Ynez. Too fast. I jumped off the sidewalk into the bushes and stumbled. The headlights' beam swiveled and smacked me in the eyes from six feet away.

Stupid driver. I had my hands on my hips and was breathing hard. I wasn't hurt beyond a scratch or two, but this blast of adrenaline would keep me from going to sleep anytime soon for sure.

Kennedy's cottage would only be a couple blocks out of the way. He stayed up late. We'd fallen into the habit of having lunch almost every day, but I hadn't seen him since we got back from L.A. on Sunday. I'd missed the seminar on Monday and wondered what Professor Barclay had to say about the results of last Tuesday's election. I would have enjoyed seeing Whittaker's reaction to FDR winning a third term. Maybe, too, I worried Kennedy would think I was avoiding him because of anger over his behavior down south. That wasn't it, though. Was it envy rather than anger? I wasn't like him, a slam-bam fellow, uninterested in women except for the chase and sex. Did I wish I were? It sure would make life simpler.

Miss Gardiner's house was dark. So *she* was asleep, anyway. I walked along the side to the back, careful not to crunch on the gravel too loudly. There. A dim glow came through the side window of Kennedy's cottage. Was he awake, then? I crept back to check.

I looked in. The single lamp in the main room was switched off, but the door to the bathroom had swung ajar and light spread from there.

Déjà vu. It was as if I were back at Stack's hideaway in Hollywood. Only the angle was different. This time I was looking at the bed, the board on the floor, not from the side but from in front. I could see the top of Kennedy's head but a woman's naked body blanketed the rest of him. Her face was lowered to his. I hadn't watched for more than a second in L.A., but here I stared.

Now Kennedy's paramour raised her head. Her lids were clamped shut. This woman had darker blonde hair, fuller breasts, and a narrower waist than the actress in Hollywood. Her tapered fingers were digging into Kennedy's shoulders. Then, as if sensing my gaze, she opened her eyes and looked over Kennedy's head. Directly at me through the windowpane.

Miriam.

PART THREE

Chapter One
October 26, 1962

In the hospital corridor, we picked up a phalanx of Secret Service men. Outside, dawn was breaking on what promised to be a breezy, clear day. It was around forty degrees, perfect for a brisk morning walk. But I was with the president and three cars awaited us when we pushed through the revolving doors of the hospital. One of the agents maneuvered me into the back seat of a black Lincoln limo for the three-block ride back to the White House.

I'd been shot at three times and hit once, but I don't think my face could have been any grayer or more drawn than his.

"You didn't have to come," I said to Kennedy. "You need your sleep."

He didn't answer.

The White House gates swung open to welcome its master home. Once inside the front door, I peeled off from Kennedy and the Secret Service and started back to my own bedroom.

"No, I want you to come with me," he said. "If you're all right, let's have some breakfast."

"I'm okay."

Doors swung open as Kennedy approached them. As I passed through, I looked behind them and saw the explanation for the magic – a man on each side holding them open. We walked up a staircase to the family living area.

Who knew Jackie smoked? When we reached a small breakfast room, there she was, lithe and lovely in a gauzy turquoise robe with a cup of coffee in one elegant hand and a lit cigarette in the other. On the tray before her were arrayed a cup of orange juice, a plate of toast, and a jar of honey, with *The Washington Post* and *New York Times* spread out on the table alongside. Her legs were crossed and a backless slipper dangled from the end of a slender foot.

"Ooh." She snuffed out the cigarette. "I wasn't expecting you."

"Ah, Jackie," her husband said, "you've heard me talk about my old Stanford friend, Nate Michaels?"

She held out her hand. I resisted the temptation to put my lips to her fingers and gave them a polite squeeze instead. "Pleased to meet you, Mrs. Kennedy."

With her now-free hand she held the collar of her robe closed. "So glad to have you visit, Mr. Michaels. But an old friend of Jack's should call me Jackie." Her voice had returned to its familiar breathy state.

"And I'm Nate."

"I saw you patrolling the halls yesterday afternoon, didn't I?"

"Yes, I was looking for Mrs. Lincoln's office."

"So nice to have you visit," she said.

The polite thing to say in response would be how nice it was to visit. I hesitated.

"He's helping me out," Kennedy said.

"How nice to have an old friend like Mr. Michaels who comes to help out when summoned," she said.

I dipped my head.

"Wait. Your ear. Did you hurt yourself?" She stood and leaned forward for a closer look. Maybe she was a little near-sighted – another flaw in the gem, hidden from the public.

"A small accident. Nothing to fret over," I said. "I'm sorry to intrude."

"No intrusion. I was just going to check on the children."

Right. That was why her coffee cup was full, her cigarette had burned down only an eighth of an inch, and the four golden-brown triangles of toast on her plate lay untouched.

"I'll send in Cook," she said to her husband.

I watched her click-clack out of the room.

The headshrinkers write about the craving for sex after a near-death experience or a funeral. They say it's a matter of embracing life and defying the fates. Maybe, but this morning that same impulse had been directed to my stomach rather than my crotch. I was ravenous.

Half an hour later, Kennedy was leafing through the newspapers his wife had left behind as I wolfed down a second three-egg cheese omelet. From behind the shield thrown up by the front section of *The Post*, he said, "I didn't anticipate this being personally dangerous. You want out?"

The Novocain in my ear was starting to wear off. I washed down a couple of the painkillers Dr. Lewis had given me.

"The Germans missed me during the War. Now the Russians have too. I guess I'm playing with house money now."

"And that means?" He lowered the paper.

"Might as well play out the hand. The shooting is good news, don't you think?"

"Probably." He slurped up some coffee without letting go of the paper. "Let's go through it. There's no reason for Volkov to want you dead, is there?"

"Well, he is KGB."

"So? That's not a reason. You didn't cheat him at gin before the War, did you?"

"We played chess. It's harder to cheat at chess."

"Did you beat him every time?"

"We split the games."

"So he didn't have a reason to come after you. No. Someone doesn't want you meeting with Comrade Maxim. Someone on the other side doesn't want me and Khrushchev communicating through the two of you."

Just what I figured, but I decided to play the contrarian. "Why on the other side? From what I saw at the ExComm, there are plenty of players on our team itching to have it out with the Soviets."

Kennedy dropped the morning's *Post* and clapped his hands. "You're learning the ways of Washington. You know, you have the kind of devious mind that would do well here. Still, it wasn't our team. The triggerman your guardian angel killed was wearing an East German suit. His teeth fillings are made of stainless steel. His gun was a Makarov."

"Trying to throw you off?"

"But they knew how to get you to come out of the White House. Who would know that on our side?"

"You, Bobby maybe, anyone who was friendly with a White House operator? No, wait. That's not right. Someone had to get that Russian receptionist to make the call. Chances are it's a player on the other side."

"Chances are?"

"Well, she could be an American spy."

"Oh, your mind is so warped, so Washingtonian. What happened to the wide-eyed law student?"

Instead of saying betrayal and war had hardened him, I said, "Let's take this as a working hypothesis, then. Someone in Moscow or on Sixteenth Street doesn't want you and Khrushchev talking to each other. They're afraid of you two settling the crisis peacefully."

"And so they want you dead," the president said.

Chapter Two

I was getting used to being lost in the White House. I'd taken two turns after leaving the breakfast room and figured the stairs up to my bedroom would be around the next corner.

I ran smack into the First Lady.

"Excuse me," I said. "I'm trying to find my way out of here."

"And you forgot to unspool the thread to find your way out." She was still in her bathrobe. Her face looked less regal and more girl-next-door without makeup than it did on the television.

"I'd been thinking the same thing. Well, I'm not looking to fight a minotaur anyway."

"You sure?" she said pointing to my ear.

"Just an accident, like I said."

"What were you and my husband discussing?"

I'd hedged on the truth once. I didn't want to do it again. "That puts me in an awkward position."

She put her hand on my upper arm. "Do you mind going back into the breakfast room with me for coffee?"

Never letting go of me, she swung open a door, and we entered the breakfast room on the opposite side from the one I'd left a minute before.

"This says something about my sense of direction. I really am a rat in a maze."

She pushed me into the chair I'd been sitting in minutes before and settled herself across from me where her husband had been. She reached into a pocket of her robe and extracted a lighter and pack of Salems.

"Don't tell Jack."

A dip of my head made me a co-conspirator.

"Jack is spending extra time with the children each night," she said. "Things must be bad. How bad?"

"Shouldn't you be asking him, Mrs. Kennedy?"

"Remember, it's Jackie." She raised her famous eyebrows.

"Why don't you ask him, Jackie?"

"All day he's under pressure. He doesn't want to bring his work back with him to the family quarters. He wants to talk to me about the kids. Right now John-John has a fever of 104. Caroline's learning to read. That's what we discuss." She took my hand. She gave me a doe-eyed smile. She used that breathy voice. "Tell me what's going on. Please, Nate."

Maybe there was a man in the country who could resist her pleading, but it wasn't me. "The Russians have missiles in Cuba."

"I'm not an idiot. I can read." She gestured toward the papers lying on the table between us.

"Let me say this. I last saw your husband in 1940. He was impressive then, more so now."

"Why didn't you see him for so long?"

"We've had our differences"

"You had differences," she repeated. "Over a woman?"

"It was a long time ago. It doesn't matter what it was over."

She knew I was prevaricating.

"It *was* a long time ago. Maybe you should let it go."

Same thing her husband had said. Had they discussed it? Were they making common cause? Who knows? Maybe they were right, but the gap between what I should do and what I could do was too wide to leap. It was safer to stay where I was. I remained mute.

"Those hurts never go away. I'm sorry for whatever he did," she said.

Why did she have to apologize for him? He'd hurt her plenty, I bet.

"What matters is what he does now," I said. "Your husband has advisors who want war. Jack knows better. With him in charge, war will only come if it must, if there's no alternative."

"Is that supposed to reassure me?" she asked.

"Yes."

She leaned in, her right hand still at her throat. "You didn't want to come here at all, did you?"

"To the breakfast room?"

"You know what I meant. Here, to Washington."

"No."

"And it's more than just a falling out with Jack. Why not?" she asked.

"This is not what I do. I'm a businessman from California."

"You served your country in the War."

"That was a long time ago," I said.

"Jack saw the War as a chance to prove himself."

"And he did."

"But not you. What did the War teach you?" She tilted her head to the side and blew out a white cloud.

"That I prefer peace."

"Jack tells me you were a war hero," she said.

"Not like him."

"That's not what I heard, but Jack embraced his experiences in the War, exploited them, got elected to Congress. You ran away from yours. Why?"

I left her question wriggling on the carpet between us like a landed fish on a boat deck.

After another deep drag, she said, "He wants me to take the children and go to our country place."

"What do you want to do?" I asked.

"I want to be here with him."

But her husband didn't want his family staying in this white house, this bull's-eye smack dab in the middle of the nation's capital. I thought of my own family in Palo Alto.

"What about your family?" she asked, as if I had spoken aloud.

"Back in Palo Alto, I have a wife and two kids."

"A wife and two kids, just like Jack. You're worried about them?"

"Of course."

"Don't you think your wife is worried about you?"

"I guess so."

"I'm not guessing. She is. Are you telling her what you're up to here?"

"Some of it."

"Do you think she could take all of it?"

"Yes."

"And how about me?"

"Your voice is soft, but you're a tough cookie."

She shook her head, snubbed out her cigarette, and stood up. She stood on her toes to kiss me on the cheek. "Thanks for listening to me. I'm glad Jack asked you back here. You're a good friend to have."

Her words brought me back to Stanford, when I'd heard Vi Roberts say almost the same thing. Again, I was listening to Kennedy's woman because he wouldn't.

Jackie reverted to her role as the nation's hostess and threw that famous shy half-smile in my direction. "Let me know if there's anything I can do to make your stay more comfortable."

Did Kennedy underestimate his own wife? Did the breathy voice, the aristocratic manner, hide her empathic intelligence even from him?

To make certain I didn't get lost this time, Jackie walked me out to the stairway.

"Go rest up. I'll bet you're going to have one stressful day."

———

I followed Jackie's advice and lay on the red and white bedspread of what ought to have been the emperor of Japan's bed, my hands folded behind my head and staring upwards at the creamy ceiling. The rays of the morning sun sliced through the window's sheer curtains. It was ten thirty and I didn't need to be downstairs for an hour.

When the War was over, I hadn't known what to do. I hadn't expected to face such a predicament, but somehow I'd found myself alive. A couple of my friends had wanted to stay in the service, but didn't get the option. I was given the choice, but said no. I wanted out. As long as the War went on, I dropped bombs on factories, power stations, oil refineries, and cities in Germany that looked just like factories, power stations, oil refineries, and cities in California – it was my job. Flying at twenty thousand feet, I hoped they would be rebuilt for better people than the Nazis. But things looked different at ground level. After V-E Day in the summer of '45, I was sent to Aachen, Cologne, and Essen to evaluate the effectiveness of aerial bombardment. When I handed out C-rations or chocolate bars to ragamuffins on the street, I couldn't help but wonder whether a bomb I'd dropped had made any of them orphans.

I ran away from war and destruction. I became a husband, father, and business executive, a man in a gray flannel suit. My original intent in going to law school had been to help save the world as a stalwart of justice. But during lectures in my first quarter back, my mind would wander away from *Marbury v. Madison* to Messerschmitts. My youthful idealism had been dropped over

Germany along with countless M-43 bombs. Three weeks into the quarter, I quit.

After trying banking for a couple of years, I stumbled into my current profession. On a superficial level, I enjoyed the challenge of selling instruments and managing men. During the War I hadn't always respected my commanding officers, but Bill Hewlett and Dave Packard were not only brilliant, they cared about each employee. They demanded and received your best. I made enough money for a comfortable life, but was I comfortable?

Now eighteen years after German anti-aircraft guns had last sent their black flowers of death to explode outside the Plexiglas cockpit of my B-17, I'd been shot at again. I thought of myself as a civilized man, but maybe I wasn't. Maybe more than one beast was penned inside my chest. The idea the world was ending sent waves of panic through my gut, but that was fear for my family. Other than that, I'd been here before, back when I'd been taking off from a small island floating off the coast of Europe, flying planes swathed in linen or aluminum through a gauntlet of German flak and fighters.

I'd told Kennedy and my wife that my place was back in Palo Alto. Was that true? Here I was again being shot at while doing my bit. Could I make myself believe again that what I did made a difference? Maybe. It sure as hell meant more than selling oscilloscopes to Douglas Aircraft. Had I been waiting for this? I'd run away from my *métier* in 1945, but now in 1962, thanks to that assassin, I was back, a soldier at war again. Maybe it was what my father's mother, who'd grown up speaking Yiddish, would have called *beshert*. Fate, destiny.

Chapter Three

"You remember looking at photos after you'd done a bombing run over Germany?" Kennedy asked.

I jerked with surprise. "I was just thinking about that a few minutes ago."

"And?"

"Sure I remember. It was like getting grades after finals."

We were walking from his office to the Cabinet Room. I'd cleaned up.

"Only the stakes were higher," the president said.

"Goddamn right. When we missed, airmen died for nothing."

"How good were you at interpreting what you saw?"

"As good as I had to be."

"I'm terrible. When I saw the first photos of the missiles in Cuba ten days ago, all I saw was countryside. Bobby's no better. He thought they were clearing for a farm. Anyway, we've got more photos coming in every day. I've got to go to this ExComm meeting. I want you to go be my eyes on the photos this morning. Go over to the NPIC. That's the National Photographic Interpretation Center."

Yesterday, I was supposed to go with him to all the ExComm meetings. Now I was going to interpret the photo interpreters. It was like he was trying to keep me busy. What was his game? Did he think I was a good luck charm?

"Okay," I said.

"They're expecting you. A car's waiting in front. When you get back, find me."

"Got it."

"Before you go, talk to Mrs. Lincoln's gal."

I watched him walk away, shoulders stooped. Bobby came around the corner and Jack wrapped his arm around him.

I slipped back to Mrs. Lincoln's area. Miss Collins was typing away. She looked up with a flustered but chipper smile. "Good morning, Mr. Michaels."

"The President told me to stop by."

"Um, apparently, you're going to be here for a while. The President figures you'll need some more clothes. If you'll tell me what you need, I'll go over to Brooks Brothers and pick them all up for you."

"Thanks, but I can take care of that."

She tilted her head and asked, "What is that on your ear?"

"I cut myself shaving."

She stared for another beat, shook her head, and went on. "The president said he was going to keep you busy and you wouldn't have time to shop for yourself."

I started to reply, but she cut me off. "You shouldn't be embarrassed. I've got three brothers at home."

"Okay. Thank you. A suit. I can't keep wearing the same one every day. I'm a 42 long with a seventeen sleeve, thirty-four waist, and thirty-two inseam."

She was taking notes. "Navy or gray? Pinstripe or plain?"

"You must have better taste than I do. You pick. And another pair of shoes. 11D. Pick those too, please." I reached back for my wallet where I always kept a blank check.

"No, no. The president told me to put it on his account."

"Just fill in the amount on the check." I made the check out to Brooks Brothers, signed it, and handed it over. I didn't want to owe Kennedy anything.

"What else?" she asked.

"Well, I would like to call the Soviet Embassy."

She gestured toward her phone.

I asked the operator to connect me.

"Hello, Comrade Leontieva. I hope you had a good night's sleep."

"Who is this, please?"

"Nathan Michaels."

"Good morning, Mr. Michaels."

"I am surprised to be talking to you again today," I said.

"Again?"

"Yes, after we spoke at five this morning."

"No, I do not start duty until eight," she said.

"You didn't call me early this morning?"

"No." The tone of her voice remained flat. She was a Soviet robot with a mechanical voice. Had someone else called pretending to be her or was she just denying being an accessory to attempted murder?

"Are you still there, Mr. Michaels?"

"I would like to speak to Comrade Volkov."

"I will take a message."

Ten minutes later I was sitting in the passenger seat of a Lincoln driving through a ratty neighborhood less than two miles from the White House. The trash was heaped in random piles, vehicles with shattered windshields squatted on the street, the sidewalks glittered with glass. The driver, a Secret Service agent, pulled up at Fifth and K in front of a car dealership called Steuart Motor Company.

"This is it," he said.

"I'm not in the market for a new Ford," I said, looking into the showroom. "The Galaxie I have at home is only a year old."

"You want to go up to the fourth floor. Mr. Lundahl is expecting you."

The entrance was past the windows of the car showroom, which jutted out from a dirty red brick building that looked like a factory. I stepped over an unshaven man in a raincoat stained by rain, mud, and sweat. His loud catarrhal snoring led me to the logical conclusion – that he was asleep – but before my hand reached the doorknob the snoring stopped and I heard, "Buddy, you got some change?" My father had always carried quarters in his pocket to give beggars and taught me to do the same. I flipped it toward him, and his hand whipped out like Giants first baseman Orlando Cepeda snaring a low throw from across the diamond. I wondered if the panhandler was some CIA agent under deep, really deep, cover. Before the door closed behind me, the snoring had resumed.

I made it past the building guard and the security turnstile that he oversaw into an elevator that creaked under the strain of lifting my hundred seventy pounds up fifty feet.

Ten minutes later I was sitting in Art Lundahl's office. He was medium height with salt-and-pepper hair a shade longer than crew-cut length. He wore what seemed to be the government-issued uniform – suit pants, white shirt, loosened tie. He had a Camel in his right hand and a mug of coffee in his left.

"So who the hell are you?" he asked in a not unfriendly tone.

"The president sent me down here."

"That's what I heard."

"Then you know as much as I do."

"God, I guess those credentials are going to have to do."

When he paused for a puff, I asked, "Why do you house your operation here?"

He exhaled a series of wispy doughnut rings. "We're close to everything – the Pentagon, the White House, the CIA – but who would ever expect to find us here in this kind of neighborhood?"

"What do the car salesmen downstairs think?"

"You mean when they see us running in and out with brief-cases guarded by guys with M-1s?"

"Yeah."

"That we must be counterfeiters." He took a slug of coffee and swirled it around his mouth as if to wash away the tobacco taste. "I think I know why you're here."

"Good. I don't."

"The president doesn't like jargon. I was trying to explain to him what it meant when a site was operational. I did a shitty job. Each Soviet site has four missile pads. We say the sites are un-occupied if they're up and ready but empty. We only say they're occupied when a missile is sitting on the pad. He wanted to know how many missiles could be fired how fast." I waited while he took another drag. It must have been twenty seconds before his mouth opened to let out the smoke it held captive. "He wants someone else to put in layman's terms what we got here. You're going to be his translator. What experience you got with recon?"

"Not much. Flew Forts in the War."

"Did you ever lead a squadron?"

"Starting in early '44."

"So you did the targeting based on photo recon?"

"Yeah."

"Okay. Let me show you what we got."

Apparently I'd passed the first test.

In the open area outside his office milled a dozen men in the same civvy uniform as Lundahl, all satisfying their cravings for caffeine or nicotine or both. Beyond them at the far end of the room, two hundred feet from where we stood, were four doors, two with green lights shining above and two with red. I squinted to cut down on the glare of the overhead fluorescents. A few were popping and crackling like loud bowls of Rice Krispies and milk.

We stopped at the end of a large flat surface formed by the tops of a row of olive drab metal file cabinets.

"You ready for your tutorial?" he asked.

"Let's go, professor."

He pointed with the lit end of his Camel at three oversized photos. I looked at a series of shots of fields, vegetation, shacks, and country lanes. Yes, they were shots of the countryside, but still not all that different from what I'd seen of the cities of Aachen, Hannover, Schweinfurt, and Berlin before my bombing runs two decades ago.

"Lazy days in the Cuban countryside."

He pointed at a magnifying glass. I picked it up and started an inch-by-inch examination. Nothing notable until I came to a series of gray rod shapes.

"Looks like the bacilli I saw under the microscope in high school biology. Missile launchers?" I asked.

"I like that. Bacilli. Disease-carrier. You got it."

"These are taken from what altitude?"

"From a U-2 flying at 70,000 feet."

I continued playing Sherlock Holmes with the magnifier. "And what are these white blotches?"

"Missile trailers."

"What's the range on these missiles?"

"They're MRBMs, medium-range ballistic missiles. Maybe 1,400 miles."

I let out my breath. Palo Alto was further from Cuba than that.

"They could reach New York, then," I said.

"Here too." He pushed another recon photo over to me.

"Looks a lot like the first one except the rods are bigger."

"They're IRBMs, intermediate missiles with a range of almost 3,000 miles."

"Shit." Now California *was* in range. It didn't make sense to me that intermediate-range meant longer than medium-range. Weren't intermediate and medium synonyms? No matter. I was looking at the very instruments that could incinerate my wife and kids and millions more.

"What does this remind you of?" Lundahl used his burning pointer to indicate a wedge hacked out of the vegetation on another photo.

In the summer I turned eleven, we'd pulled weeds out of an empty lot near the waterfront in China Basin so we could play the national pastime. "This sounds strange, but a ball field?"

"Bingo. Which means. That the troops are ...."

"Cuban."

He nodded. "And this one?" Here the flattened area was rectangular.

"Soccer field. Russians."

"Okay, you're trainable. You want a job?" he asked.

I didn't get a chance to answer. A shout came up from the reception committee by the lobby. "They're here."

With the kind of oversized leather case used for paintings or engravings dangling from his arm, a man wearing clear plastic-rimmed glasses entered the room. Three steps behind came an Air Force MP carrying a rifle. What the hell *did* those car salesmen and winos downstairs think?

"Bring them over here," Lundahl yelled out. He turned to me. "We've been looking at U-2 shots. The ones that just came in are going to be low-level."

After five minutes of looking at the new photos with the team of interpreters, I asked Lundahl if I could use the phone in his office.

I was back in two minutes. "The president's waiting for us," I told him.

Chapter Four

"Nate, have you met John McCone?" Kennedy asked from his rocking chair.

"I interrupted your meeting Wednesday, but we didn't get a chance for a formal introduction," I said with my lips formed into a simulacrum of a smile.

"John, Nate's giving me a hand here."

Behind his wire-rimmed lenses, McCone's eyes were slits. I shook his small, dry hand.

The president was rocking faster than usual. Of the four others in the Oval Office, Bobby and I were settled in the deep feathery embrace of the couch – we'd need a crane to lift us out. In front of three easels holding the oversized low-level reconnaissance photographs, Lundahl held a pointer in his hand like Leonard Bernstein an instant before the first note of a Beethoven symphony. McCone sat on the edge of a leather-backed chair between the presidential rocker and the couch.

Kennedy turned to the matter at hand. "The Russians always think they are *so* smart. A week ago Gromyko, that sonuvabitch, was in here telling us there were no Russian missiles in Cuba." He looked at his brother.

"God, I'd love to take these photos and shove them in his lying face. But Gromyko is the Soviet foreign minister," Bobby said. "What do you expect?"

"Do you think these missiles are ready to fire?" Kennedy asked Lundahl.

McCone stood up and took the pointer from his subordinate. He wanted to conduct the briefing himself. "There's a whole complex here. See, here's a missile erector for an MRBM. Here's a cable that goes over into the power source." He tapped the photo. "And there's the missile stored over in this building. We do think it's ready to go."

"Could we take them out in an air strike?"

"Any that we could see," McCone said. "They're liquid-fueled, plenty volatile. The problem is we don't see all the missiles that go with the launchers. They've moved some or hidden them. Of the six sites we've spotted all over the island, we think five are ready to go."

"What else we got?"

McCone passed the pointer back to Lundahl, who moved to the next easel. Amidst the rows and rows of Soviet tanks, he laid the tip against an oblong object with shark fins at the bottom.

"We call these FROGS, Mr. President. Solid fuel missiles. The radar truck next to it is responsible for guidance."

"What's its range?"

"Thirty miles," Lundahl answered with no hesitation.

"So it's tactical."

"Yes, sir. And it could have a nuclear tip."

"John." Kennedy turned away from the photo to McCone and let a narrow-eyed stare of his own linger for a long ten seconds. "John, if we invade Cuba, there's a good chance that these guys will use nuclear weapons against our boys?"

"Better than fifty-fifty they have nuclear tips. If they do, they'll use them. Why else have them there?" McCone spoke like a small-town bank officer foreclosing on a mortgage.

"Lundahl said these FROGs are solid fuel?" I asked.

"Yes," McCone answered without taking his eyes from his boss.

"So we'd have trouble taking them out because they're ready to go without fueling?" Kennedy asked.

"You got it, sir," Lundahl replied.

"Thanks, Art. Good work. John, you'd better get back and see what's going on."

As they left, Mrs. Lincoln brought in ham and Swiss sandwiches with Cokes. I declined and Bobby did the same.

"Tuna instead, Nate?" Kennedy asked.

"Yes, please."

Bobby said no again.

The president took a bite of his lunch and I took a sip of the drink. "You were right to get Lundahl over here PDQ," Kennedy told me. "If we'd left it to normal channels, it could have taken hours longer. Not good news, but now we know the situation. Tactical nukes with the thumb of some Soviet battalion commander on the button. Bobby, what's up with you?"

The younger Kennedy brother looked pale and his chin had sunk into his chest. "You know I've been pushing all along for taking out the missile bases, but now we find out they have tactical nukes...."

So if it had been up to Bobby, he would have stumbled over the tripwire that launched nuclear weapons. Give the guy credit for acknowledging it.

"There are two ways to do this. One is the diplomatic way." Kennedy looked at me and then continued. "That's the long shot. The other way is a combination of an air strike and invasion, which means we would have to carry out both with the probability they would use those tactical nukes."

A half minute of silence followed. I don't know how long the three of us would have sat there contemplating Armageddon if Mrs. Lincoln hadn't come back in with my tuna salad sandwich. I raised it up and put it back down without even taking a bite. Same as Bobby, I had no appetite.

Chapter Five

Like Volkov had done after our lunch yesterday, Kennedy rolled a long cigar between his fingers and took a huge puff.

"You ever read *Guns of August?*" he asked from his rocking chair.

"Barbara Tuchman's book? Not yet. It's on my nightstand at home," I replied.

"She shows how Europe stumbled into war. Tipping the first domino led inevitably to the last one falling. Destiny dictated that the death of one man would lead to millions dead."

I could tell Kennedy didn't really want to discuss European history with me. I said nothing.

"You know what's going on now?" he continued. "We've got 120,000 troops ready to land on over forty miles of Cuban beaches. The 82nd and 101st Airborne are standing by. General Howze is bitching about his men being held in ready status for too long. Bad for morale, he says. They need to fight or stand down, he says. Worse yet, word of what we saw this morning has gotten out to the Pentagon."

"So now our commanders want battlefield nuclear weapons too?"

"You got it. Invasion means nuclear war." He shook the cigar for emphasis and a shower of ash dropped. He paid no attention. As he took a long puff, I could read the word "Upmann" on a red and gold band encircling the wrapper leaves of tobacco. Cigar clenched in teeth, he continued, "I asked our generals what would happen if one, just one, nuclear missile hit a medium-sized city – Atlanta, Miami, or Dallas. 600,000 dead."

"Same as the whole Civil War," I said.

"That was a hundred years ago and we haven't gotten over it yet. You heard anything new from Volkov?"

The tip of the presidential cigar glowed red.

"No."

"Damn, it was a nice try. Well, we had to try something, anything. This is crazy, insane, that two men, sitting on opposite sides of the world, should make the decisions leading to an end to civilization."

I tried to think of the right thing to say, but he wasn't waiting on my response. My sitting there listening gave him what he needed. He was really talking to himself, blowing off steam and cigar smoke.

"What time is it?"

I looked down at the watch my father had given me when I left for the War: a Hamilton. The second hand whirled on its own inside the larger circle marked by Roman numerals. I added three hours since I hadn't changed it to East Coast time. "Seven thirty."

"Wait for me if you can. I'm going to go up and say goodnight to Caroline and John-John."

"Sure."

I went over to the humidor and cut the end off of a presidential stogie. I hadn't smoked one since 1945 and it sure wasn't an Upmann. After the War, my wife had made it clear the cigar smoking would have to stop. I watched the flame dance as I lit it with a long kitchen match. Who could blame Kennedy for wanting to spend extra time with his children at a time like this? A first deep draw on the cigar sent my mind to the twins. Didn't they deserve to have the opportunity to grow older and deal with what a long life held in store for them – love and heartbreak, hope and disappointment, adventure and tedium?

The door banged open behind me. "That didn't take long," I said.

"What didn't?" Wrong brother. It was Bobby. I turned around. He had Dean Rusk with him.

"He's saying goodnight to your niece and nephew," I said.

"I'll go get him," Bobby said, leaving me with the secretary of state, who had a sheaf of curled pages clutched in his hand.

"Would you like a cigar, Mr. Secretary?"

"No, thank you."

"Would you like to sit down?"

"No, thank you."

"What do you have there?" I asked, pointing at the pages.

"Better to wait for the president."

I was no master of small talk, but I was Dale Carnegie compared to this saturnine Georgian.

When the two Kennedy brothers returned five minutes later, they found us standing mute, ten feet apart, me with a cigar between my teeth, Rusk with his arms folded across his chest.

"So what have you got for me, Dean?" his boss asked.

"Is it okay to go ahead?" he responded. I doubted he was checking the bona fides of the attorney general. That left me.

"Pretend Colonel Michaels isn't here."

I hadn't been called that in a long time. Still, hearing my wartime rank did seem to reassure the secretary of state. He was used to dealing with the military.

Rusk waved a cable in front of him. "This is from our embassy in Moscow. It's a translation of a message written by Khrushchev."

"How do you know that?"

"It had his handwritten notes on it." Rusk was rolling from heels to tiptoes and back as he spoke.

"Okay, from the man himself then."

Kennedy took it over to his rocking chair. He read. As he finished a page, he handed it to Bobby. When he finished, it came to me.

After the preliminaries, I came to a hint of better news to come at the bottom of the first page. "Everyone needs peace: both capitalists, if they have not lost their reason and, still more, communists, people who know how to value not only their own lives, but more than anything, the lives of the peoples."

The president was two pages ahead of me and he looked as though he had ten more to go. "You can sure tell this was written by the guy who spent six hours denouncing Stalin. These Reds are so full of hot air," he said. "Just rhetoric so far."

"Keep reading, sir," Rusk said.

The pages piled up in Bobby's hand. He didn't read as fast as his brother.

"Wait, wait, wait," Kennedy said. "Listen to this. 'If assurances were given by the President and the government of the United States that the USA itself would not participate in an attack on Cuba, if you would recall your fleet, this would immediately change everything.'"

"It even gets a little better," Rusk said.

Now the president was turning over a page every half minute. He called out, "Bingo! If we pledge not to invade, then Khrushchev says, 'The necessity for the presence of our military specialists in Cuba would disappear.' So Dean, do you think this means if we promise not to invade, they'll get their troops and missiles and bombers out of there?"

"He's being a little obscure, but the department's Russian boys think it does sound that way."

"That's great news, Dean." The president clapped his hands. "Great news."

"We'll get going on a response, sir."

After Rusk left the room, Kennedy hoisted himself out of his seat and punched me on the shoulder. "You did it, you S.O.B. That meeting with Volkov paid off."

"Who knows if that's what did it?"

"This is Washington. Blame is easy to come by. Credit is rare. Take it."

"Just like you said Wednesday night. It's too early."

Chapter Six

"This sounds like one of your business deals. You always say in a good deal both sides should feel they've won," my wife was saying. "We get the missiles out and the Russians get a promise not to invade."

Just then came a quick knock on the door. It was only ten o'clock — a couple of hours earlier than the last two presidential visits.

"It's him," I said. "Gotta go."

"Good *shabbos*," she said. "Good luck too."

"Tell the boys I said good night. Good *shabbos*." I hung up. Then I called out, "Come in," wondering why Kennedy was waiting for a summons this time.

As the door opened, I expected to see him outlined against the hall lights. Instead, a suit on a hanger appeared through the opening. I waited and a few seconds later the blue pinstripes were followed by a lissome arm and then a bespectacled face.

"Kind of late to be working, isn't it?" I asked.

"I thought you might need these," Miss Collins said.

"You're right. I do. Thank you." She took a step into the room, and the door slammed behind her.

In the dim light, I saw her reach out toward me with the suit dangling from one arm and a blue shopping bag emblazoned with a golden ram from the other. I leaned around her and flicked on the overhead light.

She was wearing some kind of ivory-colored sheath dress. Like just about every woman in the country, she was taking her fashion cues from the First Lady. I relieved her of her burden. "Thank you. You okay? You're shaking."

"How did you really hurt your ear?" she asked.

"An accident this morning."

"It doesn't hurt?"

"I'm taking aspirin by the fistful."

She walked over to the far wall to examine the red wallpaper that featured Washington with a star-spangled Columbia hovering protectively over his shoulder. "This room is beautiful," she murmured.

I peeked in the bag and saw white button-downs and undershirts, socks, and two repp ties. There were even a few packs of boxers. How did she know I wore them and not briefs? Was the cleaning lady inspecting my dirty laundry and reporting to the president? I threw the shopping bag in the armoire and hung up the suit.

"This is above and beyond. You have great taste."

"You like the suit?" she asked.

"Love it." I went over to her, took her elbow, and started guiding her back to the door. She was still shivering even though, as usual on the East Coast, the room felt overheated to me. "Thank you so much."

She stopped. "The bed too." She stared at it.

"The bed?"

She ran her hand over the curve of the footboard. "The sheen of the wood .... It's beautiful too."

"The president says it's a sleigh bed on loan from the Smithsonian. I'm keeping it warm till Emperor Hirohito decides to visit."

She let me continue walking her toward the door.

Once we reached it, she shook loose and took off her glasses.

Peering at me through blue eyes not quite focused, she asked, "What's going to happen? Are we all going to die?"

"Don't know, but things are looking better."

"And I hear things. I have nightmares. We could all be gone by next week. I see …." She stopped, opened her eyes wide, and whispered, "Mushroom clouds." And then she threw her arms around me. Her hug was energetic enough to squeeze her breasts flat against my ribcage. I bent forward at the waist to make sure my groin kept a respectful distance from her midriff.

"The president is working hard to make sure there's no war," I said, too loud, into her right ear. "Things are looking better," I repeated.

Her first response was to squeeze even harder. Then she loosened her grip and raised her head. Her eyes were closed and lips parted.

I leaned down and gave her a peck on the cheek.

Not what she was looking for. She pushed me away. "I'm not very good at this, am I?" She put her glasses back on.

"At this? Like you've had experience with showdowns between nuclear powers before?"

Tears started down her cheeks. "The world might be gone by Monday. All the girls are …."

"Having flings?" I asked.

"Yeah." She lowered her head and let me go.

Proximity to death was indeed serving as an aphrodisiac.

"And you figured I was the closest available man?"

"You're nice. You talk to me."

"Listen. I flew in the War. Every time I took off, I figured I might not come back."

"So what did you do about it?"

I thought of Eleanor, the shy Englishwoman whose bed I'd shared for two years. During our time together there'd been no past and no future. Just the now, just two people huddled together to stave off the cold of loneliness. Her husband had died at Tobruk in '41. Except we found out on New Year's Day, '44, he hadn't. From that moment she had a future – but I still had not.

"I seized the moment. Like you're trying to. I understand. I know how you feel."

"So?" she asked.

"Here's the difference. I wasn't married then. Now I am. I have two kids. I have to believe in the future."

"You're saying no because you're an optimist?"

"Yeah. And because I was betrayed once when I was about your age. I can't do the same thing to my wife."

Chapter Seven

A minute after Miss Collins left, I watched the doorknob turn again.

Oh, God. I'd tried to turn her down gently. I took a deep breath.

But it was not the young intern who swung the door open. It was the president.

"Everything okay, Nate?" He strolled in and sat down on the antique bed.

"You mean besides the world being about to blow up?"

"I passed Miss Collins in the hallway. How are the clothes she picked out for you?"

"Great. Thanks for arranging that."

His mouth opened but before the word came out, the door to the Empire Guest Room banged open again.

"Goddammit, Jack. Even while I'm in town?"

Again in her turquoise robe, this time with hair in rollers, clenched fists on hips, stood the First Lady of the land. She looked around the room and even opened the closet door before letting her hands fall.

Jack put his feet on the floor and winced as he straightened up. "Ah, Jackie, we're just visiting."

"Good evening, Mr. Michaels. Nate. Nice to see you again." She tottered toward us in her backless, heeled slippers. "Shall I order up some hot cocoa?" she asked in a tone that had turned hospitable.

Just what I needed – a slumber party in my bedroom at the White House.

"Not for me, thank you," I said.

"Mr. Michaels, Nate, I apologize. I always seem to be *déshabillé* when we meet."

"No, *I apologize* for always roaming around not knowing where I am," I said.

"Don't be silly. Anyway, there's no sense Jack keeping you cooped up here in the attic like Mr. Rochester's batty wife," she said. "You'll need to come down and see the family dining room and have dinner with us. Meet the children too."

I wondered again where she'd been during the dinner party the night before last. Even if she did know about it, she didn't appear to know I'd been there.

After Jackie left, her husband slapped his thigh. "You're sure as hell not who she expected to find here."

I stood up. "You haven't grown up, have you?"

He looked at me with open-faced guilelessness. "What do you mean?"

As if he didn't know. His very calmness incited me – as it was meant to. But before I could say anything, he went on, this time with an edge to his tone. "Me? I haven't grown up? What about you nursing your little hurt from before the War? Get over it. You're married with two kids."

"So are you. That's the point."

"Who put you in charge of others' morals? It was twenty-two years ago. It's a different world now and it's not my fault if it doesn't work the way you want it to. The world *never* works the way you want it to or haven't you found that out yet? Grow up yourself."

"You're betraying Jackie, like you betrayed me."

"I betrayed you?"

"You broke the code. I was your friend. You slept with my girl."

"You weren't engaged."

"You knew I loved her."

"And I'm pretty sure she loved you too. And I tried to stay away from her because of that."

"You tried to stay away from her?"

"She came to me."

No matter whether I knew that or not. His words thundered in my skull, casting out rational thought. My heart was hammering like I had two 109s on my tail. I stood and pulled a fist back. Kennedy didn't move to defend himself, nor did he take his eyes from me.

After the time it took for three breaths, I dropped my hand and sat back down.

His eyes still on me, Kennedy said, "Do you think I wanted to bring you out here? I would rather have asked Dick Nixon for help than you. I had no choice. Volkov asked for you. I thought you could get beyond what happened. It isn't exactly a personal favor. Look at what's at stake."

For thirty seconds I breathed deep and listened to the thudding of my heart against my ribcage. Then I said, "I know what's at stake. That's why I'm here."

I unclenched my fists and sat back down on the bed. Seeing Kennedy again had opened a cage door. I knew a beast of resentment and anger and betrayal had been growling inside me, but for the first time since 1940, it had leapt all the way out of the cage and almost run amok before I could wrangle it back in.

After another minute or two, Kennedy asked – as if Jackie had never interrupted our conversation and as if we were back at Stanford in Professor Stuart's class – "What do you think is going to happen at the ExComm meeting tomorrow morning?"

I was being manipulated, but so what? I wasn't going to assault the president in the White House when he was trying to save the world. I knew that now and Kennedy had known it from the beginning. Now he waited for an answer.

"Any bomber man like me is going to wonder why we don't take out the missiles," I said.

"Before the Bay of Pigs those sons of bitches with all the fruit salad on their chests nodded like kewpie dolls, saying the operation would work, that it would be the end of Castro. I spoke to Eisenhower after the fiasco, and he asked me if I'd had everyone in front of me debating the pros and cons before I approved the plan."

"You hadn't."

"No, so this time, before I decide to send in the bombers, I'm going to hear from everyone. I'm not just going to listen to the bomber men. In fact, I'm not going to pay all that much attention to the uniforms at all. I've learned better."

"Fair enough." Okay, the last big confrontation over Cuba had taught him a lesson. If this one went as wrong as that one had, we wouldn't be around to worry about learning anything.

We talked another hour, until midnight.

On his way out, Kennedy stopped at the doorway and turned around.

"Are we okay now?" he asked.

"I'll do what I need to do."

"Like always," he said as the door swung shut behind him.

In darkness, unable to sleep, I went back to our conversation in his Stanford cottage when Kennedy told me his brother Joe was his family's crown prince. But Joe had been killed during the war, and it was Jack who inherited the throne. From there, my mind skipped to David, king of Israel, who'd been willing to betray one of his captains, have him killed, after one look at Bathsheba, the officer's wife. He suffered at God's hands for what he'd done. Was this vengeful God now punishing the president of the United States for what he'd done with Miriam? If so, I hoped the innocent would not have to suffer along with him.

Chapter Eight

I watched Kennedy breast-stroking up and down the length of the pool in the White House basement. Dave Powers, his old crony from Boston and now his companion, a valet plus, stood beside me with a heavy Turkish towel draped over his arm.

"The doc told him the swimming is good for his back," Powers said.

Kennedy grabbed the rail and emerged from the water. Twenty-two years ago he'd been wiry, even skinny. Now here he was a son of Poseidon, hair dripping, shoulders broad, chest muscular. Powers handed him the towel.

I hooked a finger under the collar of my just-out-of-the-wrapper white shirt to let some air circulate against my sweaty neck.

"That's a great mural," I said with a gesture.

"My dad gave it to me as a housewarming gift," Kennedy said as he dried off his hair. "I couldn't say no."

"The Caribbean?" I asked.

I heard a muffled "yeah" from under the terrycloth. White sails against the blue of the sea took up three walls. We seemed to be smack in the middle of someone's fantasy version of a sailor's paradise.

"You really get the sense you're there," I said. "*Feels* like we are too."

"A little steamy, you mean?" Kennedy asked. "I like the pool at ninety."

When I turned around, I could see both Powers and Kennedy against the mirrored glass of the fourth wall.

Why had I been called down here in suit and tie to sweat in this ersatz version of the tropics? "What's up?" I asked.

"You have a good night?" Kennedy asked in return.

"It took a while to get to sleep after you left."

"Did you try on your new clothes? Do they fit? Miss Collins would be glad to supply anything you want."

What did that mean? "I'm wearing the suit she picked out. It's fine," I said.

"Looks good." He laughed. "Miss Collins has better taste in ties than you do. Listen, I want you to come to the ExComm with me at ten."

"Okay, I'll be there."

He rubbed his legs with the towel for a few seconds and then looked up and said, "Good."

I turned and started back up to the White House mess for my oatmeal. That was it? That's why he had Mrs. Lincoln call me at seven thirty to tell me to come down here? Or was something else going on here? Did Kennedy have a hand in orchestrating Miss Collins's abortive seduction? If I'd slept with her the night before, would that have shown I was no better than he'd been two decades before? We'd be two sinners bound by guilt. Had he come by last night to see if I'd succumbed to temptation? This morning, was he offering me a chance to change my mind?

I took a handkerchief out of my pocket – I'd found a package of them at the bottom of the Brooks Brothers bag – and wiped my forehead. Just paranoia. Kennedy had to have more than that on his mind. Didn't he?

Chapter Nine

Secretary of Defense McNamara was plumping for night-time reconnaissance of the Soviet missile sites. They'd be lit with flares. "We have to keep the pressure up."

He hadn't yet convinced his boss when Ted Sorensen came into the room.

"What is it, Ted?" the president asked.

"This just came off the AP wire."

Kennedy read aloud. "'Premier Khrushchev told President Kennedy yesterday he would withdraw offensive weapons from Cuba if the United States withdrew rockets from Turkey.'"

Mac Bundy said, "No, he didn't. He said he'd withdraw if we promised not to invade and to end the quarantine. There was nothing about the missiles in Turkey."

"He may be putting out another letter," Kennedy said. He turned and called out toward the open door, "Pierre." Pierre Salinger, the portly press secretary with devil's eyebrows, must have been waiting outside. Kennedy waved the news ticker copy. "Pierre, is Khrushchev supposed to be putting out a letter he's written to me or putting out a statement?"

"Putting out a letter he wrote to you."

"This must be a new letter that we haven't gotten, then." He looked around the table. "Where are we with the Turks about withdrawing our missiles from there?"

"The Turks are dead set against it," one of the Pentagon team said.

"Have we talked to them?" Kennedy asked.

"Not yet. It would be extremely unsettling," answered Undersecretary of State George Ball.

"Well, this is unsettling now, George, because he's got us in a pretty good spot here. I think we're going to find it very difficult to explain why we are going to take hostile military action in Cuba when all we need to do is remove those missiles from Turkey."

"For the Turks these missiles are a matter of pride," Dean Rusk said. "We persuaded them that it was an essential requirement."

Bundy added, "It would appear we were trying to sell out our allies for our own selfish interests. That would be the view of all NATO. Now, it's irrational and crazy, but it's a terribly powerful fact."

After more comments along the same line, Kennedy held up his hand. "Listen. Khrushchev has put it out this way to cause maximum tension and embarrassment. We can say our intentions toward Cuba are peaceful, but I don't want to discuss this Turkish business publicly."

Kennedy stood and nodded toward me.

We left the Cabinet room and made our way to the Oval Office. He plopped down into his rocker and reached over to the humidor.

"Stogie?"

"No thanks."

He fiddled with the paraphernalia that cigar smoking entailed. He sliced off the butt with a brass cutter, he drew a long match up and down the length of the tobacco-wrapped cylinder, he lit the end and drew deeply. He let smoke out and then hit his left thigh with his hand. "Goddammit. Months ago I told those brass hats to get the missiles out of Turkey." He yelled out, "Evelyn." His secretary came in. "Get me Kenny."

A minute later O'Donnell, the presidential assistant, was standing in the doorway.

"Go find out the last time I told the Pentagon to have those damned missiles taken out of Turkey," Kennedy told him. "Not the first five times, only the last one."

"I remember. It was two months ago, in August. One more thing."

"Yes?"

"You were right. We did just get an official copy of another letter from Khrushchev. And they're broadcasting its contents on Radio Moscow."

"Thank you."

O'Donnell closed the door as he left the room.

"Goddammit," Kennedy said again. This time he hit the arm of his rocking chair with an open palm. "That old bear is raising the stakes. He must know the Jupiter missiles are a pile of junk, worthless."

"What do you mean?" I asked.

"They're not in hardened silos or anything. They're above ground. They're liquid-fueled. They could be destroyed hours before they were ready. They're useless as a deterrent."

"But if you remove them now, won't it look like you're yielding to Soviet threats?"

"Yeah, but I sure as hell don't want to go to war over a bunch of obsolete missiles."

"Everyone else in the ExComm seemed willing enough to."

"Well, they don't have to push the button. Have you heard anything from our friend over at the Soviet Embassy?"

"Still no."

"Not even after the shooting? What's going on? Hoover says his FBI men haven't seen him come or go from the Embassy. Well then, I guess you're going to have to go find him yourself. Get us out of this fix. Get our deal back on track."

"I'll try."

"You'll need to take some people with you. I don't want you out there on your own again."

"Have you changed your mind? Do you think Volkov is trying to kill me?"

"No. If he were, you'd be dead."

Before I could come up with a retort, a double knock came on the door and Bobby entered. "Jack," he started and then saw me. "Uh, Mr. President, one of our U-2s has been shot down over Cuba."

"Holy Mary, Mother of God." Kennedy raised his eyes upwards as if searching for divine help. Finding none forthcoming, he turned to me. "It appears McNamara isn't the only one who wants to keep the pressure up. Get out of here. Figure out how to reach Volkov."

Chapter Ten

Back in 1960 our team at HP had been a day away from the launch of a new oscilloscope. I kept calling our attorney to make sure the patent applications were filed, but I wasn't getting through, and he wasn't returning my messages. I hopped in the car and drove up to the law firm's offices in San Francisco. I told the receptionist I was there to see Mr. Barry. We were shaking hands two minutes later. "Nothing gets a lawyer's attention faster than a call saying your client is waiting for you in the lobby," he told me.

I decided to take this lesson to heart again. No phone call. Face-to-face was the way to go.

By the time I stepped out the White House door on to the driveway, a black Lincoln from the presidential fleet was waiting for me. I looked skyward before piling into the back seat. The weather was all wrong. By all rights ominous dark thunderheads should have been gathering overhead. Instead the day was cloudless with a gentle autumnal breeze, a time for innocent kite-flying, not deadly missile-firing. Maybe this was some kind of portent. Why not drop by on a lazy weekend day to see my old friend Maxim Volkov?

"You guys ready?" I asked the two Secret Service agents in the front seat as we parked on Sixteenth, blocking the driveway of the Soviet Embassy.

"Technically, sir, once we go through that gate we're not on American soil," Agent Christian, a burly, crew-cut blond, said as he cut the ignition.

"Call me Nate. And I'm not sure we're paying attention to technicalities today," I said. "You don't have to come with me."

"Afraid we do, sir," said the other agent, Bonner, who was just as large but darker-complexioned than his partner. "The director told us to treat you like you were the president."

"And that means you do what I say?"

"Mostly, sir, it means if anything happens to you, we'd better not be around to take the blame."

Having five gunners aboard a B-17 I was piloting hadn't made me feel much safer, but I had never told them that. I didn't tell these two either. "Thank you. Let's hope it doesn't come to that."

I fumbled a little getting out of the back of the car. What in the hell was some Detroit engineer thinking when he designed a Lincoln's back door to swing open from the middle?

With the shoulders of the two agents rubbing against my own, we strode up to the Embassy door. I'd bet Bonner and Christian were carrying enough firepower to storm the gates if all else failed. I swung the brass knocker against the wood.

Ten seconds waiting. No response. I tried the knob. Locked. Figured. It was Saturday after all. Tried again. Banged harder and longer. Still nothing.

"Let's go home," I said.

We'd almost made it back to the car when we heard the door creak open.

I turned and took a step back. "Ah, Miss Leontieva. You do work weekends."

The glacial white of her face made her appear a specter amidst the shadows.

"Yesterday I delivered your message to Comrade Volkov."

Maybe the voice did sound different from the siren who'd tried to beckon me to my doom.

"We came by to see if he's in now."

"Of course." She pronounced "of" as though it were the word "off."

"Will you tell him we're here?"

"But he is not. As you said, it is the weekend."

"Would you give him another message for me, please?"

"I will try."

"Tell him to meet me at the Bernard Baruch Bench in Lafayette Square at three o'clock."

"I will try." The door closed.

"Nice talking to you," I said to the oak planks.

Once back in the Lincoln, Bonner asked, "Do all Soviet women look like Princess Aura from Planet Mongo? You know, from Flash Gordon?"

"You and your sci fi," Christian told him. Then he turned to me. "Where to, sir?"

Chapter Eleven

Two hours later I was sitting on the bench in Lafayette Square where Bernard Baruch was reputed to have come up with sage advice for whoever was in residence across the street in the White House. If he'd left behind a crumb of inspiration, I couldn't find it.

A man in a khaki golf jacket and a woman with a Kodak Brownie in her hand were shepherding two look-alike boy toddlers toward the famous slatted seat. Seeing twins made me smile, but like a dozen others who'd approached us, the family of four veered off toward the statue of Lafayette before getting within fifty feet. I looked to my right and then left. Seeing Bonner and Christian's bulk on either side of the bench, squinting as they turned their heads from side to side, would scare most anyone away.

"You two are not doing much for the local tourist economy," I said. No response forthcoming from Agents Bonner and Christian. No ideas forthcoming from Mr. Baruch. I was on my own. I looked down at my wrist. Three thirty. I'd waited long enough, but had no desire to head back to the White House and report I'd failed to get in touch with Volkov. I'd give him ten more minutes.

I spent the time staring at the minute hand sweeping around the face of my dad's old Hamilton. One, two, three, four, five.

"Okay, boys, let's go." I stood. Bonner and Christian were still looking around, so I did the same. Off to our right, a couple of men in overcoats were approaching us from Jackson Place, the street that ran along the west side of the square. I'd rather have given up the bench to the family with twins. There was the White House floating on the lawn across Pennsylvania Avenue. Seven or eight people were cutting through the park.

"Down."

A hand grabbed my shoulder and pushed me back over the bench where I landed on my shoulder just as I heard a gunshot. The bench's top slat shattered. Arms extended, the two agents were firing toward gun flashes coming from a copse of trees. Still shooting, they came around to the back of the bench with me.

Bonner's left arm was spurting blood from above the elbow even as he fired with his right. My estimate – he was about a minute from going into shock. I'd had a ball-turret gunner with the same kind of wound – he hadn't made it. Now, Christian was screaming into his walkie-talkie.

How long could it take until the cavalry arrived? The White House was across the street, for God's sake. I pulled off my right shoe and took a barely worn Brooks Brothers navy sock and wrapped it around Bonner's upper arm and knotted it tight. Better the chance of infection than the certainty of bleeding to death. The crimson splotch on his jacket arm kept spreading but the spurting stopped. Christian kept firing all the while.

I'd been shot at plenty 20,000 feet above France, Holland, and Germany, but a thousand feet from the White House? Bonner started firing again. A bullet shattered another slat of the bench and I felt another hit above my hairline. Why wasn't I dead? Oh, just a splinter, no bigger than half a toothpick. I yanked it out. Bonner's gun had gone quiet. Shit. A splinter had hit him too, but not a small one. Bonner had a jagged piece of bench four inches long sticking out of his neck above his

Adam's apple. I watched his hand go up to it. The end of the shard quivered in time with his pulse. On the third beat, he fell to the ground.

Christian looked down at his partner and then yelled to me out of the side of his mouth, "Can't wait for help." He fired a few times. "You scram. Get the hell outta here. Head toward H Street."

Bonner was looking up at us, blood pumping out of the hole in his neck, gurgling, drowning in his own blood. Nothing to do for him. I uncurled the fingers holding his automatic and fired in the general direction the bullets were coming from.

"Take the gun, but get the hell outta here," Christian shouted. "Go."

I looked down at Bonner. Dead. I'd never had to parachute out of my plane during the War, but that's what I felt like I was doing as I crouched and ran for a thicket of bushes.

Made it. Christian was holding his own.

As I turned to run to the street, I saw *him* again. In a crouch behind a tree twenty feet over, the man in the trench coat and dark glasses had the barrel of his gun pointing right at my face. A dead man. I was a dead man.

Then he turned and fired at my assailants. Who was this guy? Was he even real? As he slammed another magazine into his gun, he turned toward me again, and I saw my own small reflection in the mirrored lenses of his aviator glasses. He jerked his head toward the street indicating I should keep going. I straightened up and ran toward the north side of the park. A bullet hit a tree as I passed it. More firing. Had Christian finished off the man hunting me? I heard sirens now. Help was on the way. The gunshots grew scattered. I emerged on H and took a step into traffic.

A Pontiac slammed on the brakes and I watched the eyes of the gray-haired woman behind the wheel widen, either because she'd almost killed me or because she saw the gun and feared I would kill her. I hopped back onto the sidewalk. Two sets of arms grabbed me from behind. "Michaels," one of them said. I kicked back and hit one on the knee. A curse in Russian. I tried to swing my right hand holding the gun around. No go. An arm came across my throat and cut off my air. Caught.

Chapter Twelve

I didn't lose consciousness, not completely. I felt myself being frog-marched and then a car door opened, and I was shoved into the back seat. Tires squealed. A few seconds later a foot hard on the brake flung me onto the floor. That dispelled most of the brain haze.

I had my hand at my own throat now and pulled oxygen into my lungs in a huge gasp. Then another. From my hands and knees, I saw a pair of shiny cordovan shoes. Each breath was bringing in more of the distinctive odor of cigars smoked, cologne worn, and baths skipped. I looked up.

"Hello, Nathan," Volkov said.

Duty had trumped friendship. "Back for another try?" my voice rasped. He reached down his meaty arm and hoisted me back onto the seat next to him.

"Another try?" he asked.

I tried the door handle. Locked. A thuggish man stared at me from the passenger seat. Turning back to Volkov, I asked, "Your man missed me yesterday and then again in the park just now. Are you going to finish things off?"

"Your accusation hurts me, Nathan," Volkov said. "Your father was my brother."

I replied in a voice laced with sarcasm. "But Uncle, what do family relationships mean compared to the success of the Revolution?"

He said something in Russian to the man in the passenger seat. He passed Bonner's gun back to me. I stared at it, realizing the haze hadn't completely lifted yet.

I breathed in and out at least a dozen times before I said, "Those men in the park were not yours." Volkov had not betrayed me. He was just late as always.

When he smiled, a stainless steel incisor shone. "No," he said.

"One of them wears a trench coat and sunglasses?" I asked.

He tilted his head. "No, I told you. Not mine. Not KGB."

"He was firing at the assassins."

"Not mine," he said again.

"Okay." Who the hell was that guy in the trench coat? Minder? Protector? Watcher?

"You are missing shoe," Volkov said.

I looked down in surprise. One of my two new Brooks Brothers shoes was back by the park bench. The matching sock was wrapped around the arm of the dead-by-now Bonner.

"One of the Secret Service agents with me was killed," I said.

"Unfortunate. Accept my apologies, but we are trying to save millions."

I fingered the bandage on my ear. "Did you know that someone called yesterday morning and said she was Miss Leontieva? She told me you wanted to see me." He rotated his hand to indicate I should keep going. "Miss Leontieva told me she didn't call."

"She did not," he said.

During the War, things were as they seemed. I flew a plane, the Germans tried to shoot me down before the bombs were released. Deadly but straightforward. Now the stakes had gone up, even as the rules of the game became more byzantine.

"So someone is following me, but we don't know who he is even if he's trying to save my ass. Someone is calling me, but we don't know who she is even though she's tried to get my ass killed."

"This is world where I live," he said with a Slavic shrug that conveyed a matter-of-fact fatalism fostered by the arbitrary purges of his homeland. "Did you know you have cut on head?"

"It doesn't hurt."

Volkov said something in Russian to the man in the passenger seat in front. Back came a first aid kit, an American one with a big red cross on the white box.

"Lean to me," he said. He had a cotton ball with some orangey liquid in his hand and dabbed where I'd pulled out the splinter.

"Shit." I jerked back in response to the intense burn in my scalp. "What kind of Russian torture juice is that?"

He grabbed me closer by the shoulder and dabbed some more. "Don't be baby. Is Merthiolate, good American antiseptic. Has stopped bleeding." He leaned back to admire his nursing skill. "No infection now. This other shot came close." He was gazing at my ear.

"The man in the trench coat killed him."

"I wish I could take credit. Tell me, it was because of you the president went to hospital yesterday morning?"

"Yes." Someone on his team, apparently not the man in the trench coat, was keeping an eye on the White House.

"Ah. Navy training. A good officer takes care of men. Are people in president's cabinet who want war? In Pentagon?"

"Aren't there people in the Presidium who want to use your missiles in Cuba now?"

"You answer a question with a question? All right. So are warmongers on both sides, but you and me, we are friends. We have common purpose."

As the car crawled along Q Street in Georgetown, I reached over the back of the seat to shake hands. "Friends," I said. "With a common purpose *and* common enemies."

"On your side it must be Air Force generals. They have bombs and missiles and must want to use them."

Practically the same analysis Kennedy had made. Maxim had LeMay pegged. "You guess that because your military wants to use its bombs and missiles?" I asked.

"Perhaps."

"Where have you been?"

"Since lunch with you, I move around."

"Someone wishes to kill you as well?"

"One cannot be too careful."

"Who *might* be trying to kill you, then?"

"The same people who try to kill you."

"And that would be?" I asked.

"GRU."

"Who?"

"Military intelligence."

"Russian military intelligence is trying to kill me?"

"Yes. They are powerful group. Even First Secretary cannot enter GRU headquarters in Moscow without going through security screening. They have never been friends of Volkov."

"Why's that?"

"I told GRU Whittaker Chambers was unstable." He tapped a finger against his forehead. "GRU recruits him anyway. I am not forgiven for being correct."

"Good thing for us."

"Perhaps. Let me tell you situation now. Castro does not want missiles withdrawn. He sent letter to Nikita Sergeyevich – first secretary, Khrushchev – demanding he drop bombs on America."

"And there are military men on your side who agree?"

"Most definitely. What better time to vanquish imperialism than when missiles only 150 kilometers from your country? And Castro, he is dog with rabies. He wants vengeance for Bay of Pigs."

"He wants vengeance? You mean he wants to die. One of our planes was shot down over Cuba today. There's strong pressure on the president to give an order to retaliate if another of our planes is

fired upon. That could lead to a chain reaction very hard to stop."
I waved my hands. "*Ka-boom.*"

"I understand."

"I have spoken to the President about our last conversation. He says if the missiles are removed, the United States will not invade Cuba. It appeared Khrushchev agreed."

"He will announce this on the television?"

"He will, after your country stops all work on deploying the missiles. Work must stop now and then the missiles must be withdrawn."

"And what of your missiles in Turkey? Even Mr. Walter Lippmann suggested a swap of Cuban missiles for Turkish missiles in newspaper last week."

"I don't care whether it was Lippmann or Lenin who mentioned a swap," I said. "It is unacceptable today, tomorrow, and forever."

He spread his hands out. "No reason to be angry. I am only a bureaucrat. Military is demanding removal of your missiles from Turkey."

So that's why Khrushchev had added to his demands.

"The president cannot make such a promise without undercutting NATO," I said.

Let him think we are giving up a lot.

"Of course, my friend," Volkov said.

"Of course, what?"

"If missiles are removed from Turkey, it is victory for Soviet people. It unties noose that surrounds motherland. If we must fight, we have forces in Cuba."

I remembered what my wife had said last night. The Russians needed to win too.

"President Kennedy gave the orders for the missiles in Turkey to be dismantled in August before the current crisis even began. He was ready to remove them without threats. He cannot remove them if threatened."

"Ah." Volkov rubbed his hands. "And without threats when will your country withdraw them?"

"Within four or five months." I presumed that removing missiles from Turkey combined with the promise not to invade Cuba would let Khrushchev position the settlement as a Soviet victory. And our side could say we were going to remove them anyway. We *would* both win this way.

"I will pass on what you have said."

"How can I reach you?"

"I will call." Volkov reached down and unlaced his glossy shoes. He handed them to me.

"What are you going to do without shoes?"

"I insist."

"Thank you."

I slipped the right one on my sockless foot and tied it tight. His foot was a couple of sizes longer and wider than mine. The thickness of the wool sock on my left foot made the other shoe fit a little better.

He dropped me off at the West White House gate. One hundred fifty yards ahead, I could see a traffic jam of ambulances and police vehicles on the piece of Pennsylvania Avenue closest to the Baruch Bench.

"Hello, Mr. Michaels," the guard said as he waved me through.

Even as I trudged in my ill-fitting footwear along the drive back into the White House entrance, I kept looking over my shoulder at the mess in Lafayette Square.

A horn tooted. I'd almost walked right into the grille of a Lincoln limousine. I scooted to the side. As it rolled by, the back window opened and a hand emerged. I reached for it and squeezed. "Thank you and good luck, Nate," came the breathy words from the First Lady. I could see Caroline playing peekaboo with John-John at the other end of the back seat.

"You're going away for the weekend?"

"Yes, like I told you. Jack thought we should go to Glen Ora."

Her husband was sending his family to their weekend retreat in rural Virginia – away from what was bound to be ground zero in case of a nuclear attack. I could see two more cars behind them that must be filled with Secret Service agents. When I tried to let go of her hand, she squeezed my fingers harder.

"Help him," she said.

"I'll try."

"God bless," she said and let my hand go, but was still staring at me when the dark tinted window rolled up and covered her face.

Chapter Thirteen

"Let me start my proposition over again," the brilliant and brilliantined Robert McNamara was saying as Mrs. Lincoln ushered me into an ExComm session.

The presidential chair at the head of the table in the Cabinet Room was empty, but I took a seat behind it anyway. McGeorge Bundy stared at me as if about to ask me to leave. He was, after all, the president's national security advisor and who the hell was I? He shook his head in what could have been impatience but probably was disgust and looked back at McNamara.

"We must be in a position to attack quickly," McNamara was saying. "We've been fired on today. We're going to send surveillance aircraft in tomorrow. Those are going to be fired on without question. We're going to respond. We're going to lose airplanes every day. You can't maintain this position very long. So we must be prepared to attack Cuba quickly. That's the first proposition."

He paused and looked around the room. So did I. Like their boss, Bobby Kennedy and Ted Sorensen were MIA. Then he resumed his exposition, put forward in the same matter-of-fact tone he must have used to go over the balance sheets at Ford Motor Company.

"Now, the second proposition. When we attack Cuba, we are going to have to go with an all-out attack, and I personally believe that this is almost certain to lead to an invasion."

Was I too late? Was this what Kennedy worried might happen? Would some future historian — if there were a future — write that shooting down the U-2 was the domino that brought on World War III just as the assassination of Archduke Ferdinand had inexorably led to the First World War?

"The third proposition," McNamara said, "is that if we do this and leave those missiles in Turkey, the Soviet Union probably will attack the Turkish missiles. And the fourth proposition is, if the Soviet Union attacks the Turkish missiles, we must respond."

The door opened and Ted Sorensen stuck his head in. He caught my eye and crooked his index finger to beckon.

As I left the meeting, Bundy was stating the obvious. "It doesn't look good."

After he closed the door, Sorensen grabbed me by the arm. "What a mess. The president wants you now."

We passed by Mrs. Lincoln's cubbyhole, which separated the Cabinet Room and the Oval Office. I didn't even have the chance to reply before we entered the room where the president and his brother awaited. Bobby stopped whatever he was saying in mid-sentence. Jack had his elbow resting on the arm of his chair and his chin pressed into his palm. I couldn't read him.

"What's going on in there?" the president asked.

"The defense secretary is like a chess player looking ahead ten moves," I said.

"And the endgame is nuclear war?"

"It's only words right now."

"So what the hell went on with you this afternoon?"

I told him.

"So it was the GRU," he said after I'd finished.

"That's what Volkov thinks."

"Well, we got one of them. God, I'm sorry Fred Bonner had to die out there in the Park."

"Me too."

"You know those agents are trained to sacrifice their lives for whoever they're protecting?" he asked and turned his gaze from the ceiling and to my face. If he was trying to fan the flames of guilt burning in my gut, he succeeded. "Even though Bonner died, I think your being attacked again by the GRU is a good thing, maybe the only good news we have."

"Go on," I said.

"If it's the GRU, it's because the Soviet generals want war."

"That's Volkov's reasoning too."

"They were surprised by the German invasion in '41 just like we were by the Japanese at Pearl Harbor. They're not going to yield first move advantage again if they can help it. Plus they have Castro egging them on. It confirms what we thought before – if they were sure of war, they wouldn't be worrying about your trying to stop it."

During the War, the Germans built fake factories to fool Allied bombers into dropping their load on them. Was that what I was now, a cardboard agent intended to attract enemy fire?

"So the peace party in the Kremlin must have some juice," I said.

"I'll bet Khrushchev is no crazier about a nuclear war than I am. I've been across the table from him. You think letting them know the missiles will come out of Turkey in a few months will work?"

Bobby responded before I did. "Or is this guy Volkov leading us on, hoping we will let our guard down? We need to take a tough line."

"Before you got here, Bobby suggested we go through official channels to make sure our message gets through," the president explained. "He's got Dobrynin coming into his office."

"The Russian ambassador?"

"Yeah," Bobby said. "It can't hurt and might help."

"What're you going to tell him?" I asked.

"Same old song, that if the missiles don't come out, it will mean war," the president said. "If they do come out, there would be no reason to invade." He turned to his brother. "On top of that, Bobby, I want you to let slip that we are going to stick to our plan and take those missiles out of Turkey in the next few months."

"Isn't that giving in to their threats?" Bobby asked. His tone was almost defiant. He was the attorney general and the president's brother, his go-to guy, his alter ego. I worked in electronics in California and hadn't been in contact with the president for over two decades. Bobby must have seen me as an interloper. And now that he'd been told to follow my lead with Dobrynin, what was I now? A Rasputin?

"No, because we were going to do it anyway," the older brother retorted. "Make sure he knows that and make sure he knows that we were never going to announce that publicly and still won't." Kennedy turned to me. "Bobby's right. We need to go through official channels as well as through Volkov. If Khrushchev hears our message from both the KGB *and* the Foreign Ministry, it should give him more ammo to deal with his generals."

Mrs. Lincoln stuck her head in. "Telephone, Mr. President." He started and stared. "It's your wife." He relaxed and picked up the phone. "Hello, Jackie. How did the kids do on the drive?"

Bobby stood and Sorensen made a futile first attempt to follow. Then he threw his arms forward and generated enough momentum to get him up and out of the overstuffed couch. The two left through a small side door.

Funny that in the cold war between communism and capitalism, between dictatorship and democracy, generals on both sides would be thinking one way while the two heads of government would be thinking the other. More support for Kennedy's cynical view of governmental affairs – it doesn't matter where you stand, it matters where you sit.

As I ended my musings, Kennedy was asking Caroline about Macaroni, which I eventually figured out was a pony, not a dinner entrée. He held up a hand telling me to wait.

While he was still talking to his daughter, a silver-haired man carrying a doctor's black bag strolled in unannounced. Kennedy nestled the phone under his ear. The doctor rolled up the president's left sleeve and reached into the bag. He came out with the kind of menacing hypodermic Dr. Zamvil in Palo Alto used to give my twins their booster shots. He jabbed the needle into Kennedy's arm and pressed the plunger. The injection could not have been painless, but if the president winced, I didn't spot it. He continued chatting away. The doctor swabbed where the shot had pierced the skin and rolled down the presidential sleeve. The doctor shook a multi-colored collection of pills into Kennedy's outstretched right hand. Kennedy threw them back against his throat and chased them down with the water from a glass that sat on the desk next to a pewter pitcher. There were enough pills to swallow that this exercise had to be repeated another time. The nonchalant, practiced manner of both Kennedy and the doctor indicated this *pas de deux* had been rehearsed many times. The doctor waved at Kennedy, who was still talking on the phone, and walked out.

When I'd seen Jack having sex with that starlet in Hollywood, he hadn't treated it as an invasion of privacy, maybe because there'd been no real intimacy involved. Now he'd let me see him take in enough drugs through arm and mouth to stock a small-town pharmacy. Why? Did he trust me to keep my mouth shut? Had to be. If the American people knew their commander-in-chief was trying to deal with Soviet missiles in Cuba while all those drugs flowed through his bloodstream – well, it wouldn't be acceptable. And he knew I would say nothing. Just one more thread binding me in a web of complicity.

"Okay honey, I'll talk to you tomorrow night." He hung up the phone and turned to me. "So we need to figure out…."

"Are you sick?" I interrupted. "That seemed like a lot of medicine."

"No, no. It's my back, then there's war injuries, plus vitamins that are good for my stamina. I need stamina now, don't I?"

"I guess I took my share of Benzedrine during the War," I said with a shrug.

"Listen, the ExComm isn't working, too many people," Kennedy said. "We met for three and a half hours this afternoon and got nowhere." He leaned forward on his rocker. "In a small group you can come up with good ideas. Like taking the missiles out of Turkey without saying it was a quid pro quo."

"McNamara thinks that taking the missiles out of Turkey would be the end of NATO," I said.

"To hell with that. Leaving them in might be the end of millions of people."

"O'Donnell said you'd ordered them out two months ago."

"Damned bureaucracy. I'm president, but it doesn't matter. Commander-in-chief, maybe, but I sometimes think I had more authority in a PT boat."

Chapter Fourteen

"Shooting down our plane is an extremely serious turn of events," Bobby told the nondescript, balding Ambassador Dobrynin in a hushed tone that vibrated with restraint.

"Your plane was flying over sovereign territory. Cuba has the right to protect itself...."

I watched Bobby lean across the massive desk in his ballroom-sized office in the Justice Department building a block from the White House. The Attorney General was slight, but Dobrynin moved back as if Bobby were a rabid dog about to leap over the desk and tear at his throat. Me? I was fifteen feet away in a dimly lit corner doing my best to fade into a wall decorated with children's finger paintings and stick drawings.

It had been Jack who suggested I attend the meeting with the Soviet ambassador. Bobby had retorted he knew Dobrynin well and even had hosted him at Hickory Hill, his Virginia estate. They understood each other and a one-on-one meeting might work better. "Don't worry," his brother had told him. "Nate knows how to keep his mouth shut. I bring him into the ExComm meetings because I want another pair of eyes and ears in there to give me his impressions. I'm not saying you have to take him. I'm suggesting it's a good idea, and it's worked for me."

Bobby gave Jack an I-surrender shrug. He knew he'd been outmaneuvered. If the country's chief executive counted me as a satisfactory advisor, how could the attorney general not?

"Anatoly, I'm not here to argue international law with you," Bobby retorted. He was out of his chair, supporting his weight on hands splayed on the desktop. I had to strain to hear Bobby's soft voice which so contradicted his aggressive body language. "Here's the point. If we had not been violating Cuban airspace, we would have believed you when you told us there were no Russian missiles in Cuba."

Bobby waited for an answer from Dobrynin. When none came, he plowed ahead. "But you need to understand what's going on here. If the Cubans shoot at our planes again, then we are going to shoot back. That's fact. And once we do fire, a chain reaction will start that will be very hard to stop."

"Why should it be hard to stop?" Dobrynin sat hunched in his chair. His tone was aggressive, but his posture was submissive – the opposite of the attorney general's wild-beast-about-to-pounce body language and voice of reason.

"We're determined to get rid of the Soviet bases in Cuba."

"By bombing them?"

"If need be. And if we do bomb them, Soviet personnel will die."

"And then we will retaliate."

"That's the chain reaction I was talking about. A real war will begin. Millions of Russians and Americans will die. We want to avoid that any way we can."

"You are issuing an ultimatum?"

"No. It's a request. The president is sending a letter directly to First Secretary Khrushchev. It should arrive tonight." Bobby took a couple of carbon copies out of his jacket pocket and glanced over them. "The president says he understands the first secretary's proposals to be as follows: You will remove weapon systems from Cuba with suitable safeguards. In return we will end the quarantine against Cuba and give assurances against an invasion."

"What about Turkey?" Dobrynin asked.

I held my breath.

"If that is the only obstacle to an agreement, then the president doesn't see any insurmountable difficulties in resolving this issue."

"Mr. Attorney General, Bobby, what does that mean?" The ambassador spread out his hands.

"The president ordered the missiles removed last August and they will be. We can't announce this right now or it will look like we withdrew the missiles under pressure. If the NATO countries think we won't stand up to your government, well, that would seriously tear NATO apart."

What would the Soviet Union like better than tearing NATO apart? I wondered. Wasn't that why they sought to tie the presence of their missiles in Cuba to the Jupiters in Turkey? I looked at Dobrynin through the gloom. I saw crevasses running along his forehead, but no smile. If these two adversaries were playing poker, neither much cared for his hand.

"When would the missiles be removed from Turkey?"

"Within four to five months."

"What will you do to control your generals?" Dobrynin asked.

"Lots of our generals are itching for a fight, but our president is the commander-in-chief and they understand that. I worry much more about Russian generals who are out of control."

"I beg your pardon?"

"We are not pleased to find GRU assassins operating in our nation's capital."

"What?" Dobrynin's surprise seemed unfeigned but then his boss had lied right to the president's face about the presence of missiles in Cuba just two weeks before.

"Ask Maxim Volkov."

"I beg your pardon?" Ostensibly, Volkov worked for Dobrynin. In the past few days I'd learned that the head of the KGB in the United States answered only to its chairman, Khrushchev's man Vladimir Semichastny. And neither the KGB nor the Embassy had any control over the GRU. According to Volkov, Khrushchev himself had perilously little.

"No matter. Anatoly, what the president would like back from the first secretary is a clear answer to his letter by tomorrow. And please, not another rambling letter that will tie our State Department in knots trying to interpret it and drag all this out past the brink."

The attorney general stretched out a hand and shook Dobrynin's. The meeting was over. It had lasted less than fifteen minutes.

"Anatoly," the Attorney General called. The ambassador turned around in the doorway to hear Bobby's parting words. "There's very little time left. Events are moving too quickly."

Chapter Fifteen

Bobby and I found his brother with Dave Powers in the White House's upstairs living room.

Powers was cutting into a chicken breast on a plate balanced on his lap. Jack was balancing a picture book on his lap and reading into the telephone.

> *The Little Red Hen did not know whether the bread would be fit to eat, but – joy of joys! – when the lovely brown loaves came out of the oven, they were done to perfection.*
>
> *Then, probably because she had acquired the habit, the Red Hen called: "Who will eat the bread?"*
>
> *All the animals in the barnyard were watching hungrily and smacking their lips in anticipation, and the Pig said, "I will," the Cat said, "I will," the Rat said, "I will."*
>
> *But the Little Red Hen said, "No, you won't. I will."*
>
> *And she did.*

"Good night, sweetie," he finished. "You listen to Mummy now and go right to bed." He hung up the phone with exaggerated gentleness and looked at Bobby, then me, then Powers. "You know, we might have fucked up this world and if things continue to spiral down, we're going to get what we deserve. But what about the innocent children everywhere in the world whose lives would be wiped out in a war?" He breathed out. "Dave, hand me the opener."

We watched while he used the corkscrew to open a bottle of white wine. He played host and poured glasses for all of us. Then he raised his own and said, "To what really matters: a better world for our children." We were sitting around a coffee table with a hot plate in the middle. We clinked the rims of our glasses.

A moment later Jack asked me, "Were you thirsty or did you just want to make sure the toast came true?"

I looked blankly back at him.

"Your glass," he said. "It took you two gulps to empty the whole thing. That was good wine too. You should savor it."

I had no memory of even having drunk it. I blinked and then ran my tongue over my teeth. Yes, the tang of a Riesling did linger. "I promise I'll sip the next glass," I said and held the crystal goblet out for a refill.

"Can you spare an extra leg of that chicken?" Bobby asked, eyeing the cut-up fowl on the hot plate. "I'm starved."

We drained the bottle of wine and started another one. Knives and forks stripped the chicken bones of flesh as Bobby recounted the meeting. When he finished by telling his brother of his demand for an answer by tomorrow, Jack looked up.

"God, Dave. The way you're eating up all that chicken and drinking up all my wine, anybody would think it was your last meal."

"The way Bobby's been talking, I thought it *was* my last meal," Powers answered. Kennedy laughed and slapped him on the back. No wonder he kept Powers around.

Neither Bobby nor I gave more than a weak smile, but then we'd been in there with Dobrynin and the other two had not.

Chapter Sixteen

This time the president stood outside the bathroom in my suite while I emptied my bladder of the two glasses of wine.

"Can't hear you," I said.

In the mirror over the sink I saw him move closer and lean against the jamb. "Dobrynin understood time was running out?" he called. This time his voice came in loud and clear over the sound of my stream hitting the toilet water.

"Yes. Bobby conveyed that we were reluctantly determined."

"That's good. 'Reluctantly determined.'"

"Dobrynin is afraid you won't be able to hold back the generals much longer."

"Good."

I flushed and zipped my pants and nodded to the likeness of James Monroe hanging over the toilet to excuse any discourtesy for pissing right in front of him.

"Any problems?"

"Bobby said that any linkage between our missiles in Turkey and theirs in Cuba would lead to the end of NATO."

Kennedy and I stared at each other in the mirror. I turned on the water to wash my hands.

"You're afraid that the Russians would find that too tempting to pass up?" This time Kennedy spoke loud enough for me to hear over the running water.

I shrugged. As I turned around, I threw a hand up and caught a hand towel two inches before it smacked me in the face.

"Nice catch," he said.

"Self-defense," I said as I dried my hands.

"Self-defense – that's what we're talking about here, isn't it? Bobby did fine. He knows what I'm thinking, what I'd do. It's almost nine. ExComm time again."

Chapter Seventeen

While we'd been eating and drinking, the situation outside the sanctuary of the family quarters had been going to hell.

Rusk brought us and an inner circle of the ExComm up to date. Soviet surface ships were approaching our Navy's quarantine line around Castro's island as if to rush it. A Soviet submarine, probably carrying nuclear weapons, was trying to sneak under it.

To make certain the Russians knew how close they were to hitting the trigger point, Adlai Stevenson had proffered a formal map of the interception line to Soviet Ambassador Zorin at the United Nations. But Zorin took a step back as the former presidential nominee handed it over, and together they watched the paper float to the floor. Neither moved to pick it up.

Also at the UN, the Secretary General, U Thant, had received an answer from Castro to his appeal for a temporary standstill on construction of the missile sites. Castro had flatly refused and demanded the end of the quarantine.

The debate around the Cabinet table moved to whether there should be reconnaissance overflights of Cuba tomorrow even after the downing of the U-2. General Taylor said, "The Chiefs recommend we go back with six planes tomorrow, picking out targets that have less anti-aircraft protection. We want to verify that work in the missile sites is still going on, and also to prove we're still on the job."

After a few minutes' discussion, it was agreed we'd send the planes the next day.

Kennedy said, "If they fire at our planes tomorrow morning and we haven't got a satisfactory answer back from the Russians, we ought to put out a statement that we consider the island of Cuba an open territory and take out all the SAM sites tomorrow afternoon. As soon as all the missiles are taken out we'll invade. Monday maybe, by Tuesday for sure."

When I stared at my watch, I could never see the hour hand move, but move it did. It had been moving in the same inexorable way toward nuclear confrontation since I'd been in D.C. Now, though, the hour hand was speeding toward hostilities as if I'd pulled out the watch stem and started twirling it.

The talk around the table was no longer concerned with how to preserve peace, but how to prepare for war. The president thought our NATO allies ought to be warned right away about its imminence. He told Rusk, "In order to prepare for a disaster in Berlin or someplace, you ought to be saying to them that the situation is deteriorating. And that if we take action in Cuba, we think there will be reprisals in Europe."

Heads bobbed up and down around the table.

"John, you hearing anything different?" Kennedy asked McCone, the head of the CIA.

"I'm worried about leaks," he said. "Did the Soviets know when the U-2 they shot down was coming? I don't want them to know that we're planning on hitting them tomorrow." He flicked his eyes toward me.

Kennedy caught it. "You think Mr. Michaels here is letting the Russians know what we're up to?"

"Well...."

"Well, what?"

"He's been meeting with the KGB."

Bingo. About half the time I watched *Perry Mason* on TV, I had a flash of who the murderer was. Same feeling this time. "Excuse me, Mr. President," I said. "May I ask a question?"

He didn't much like being interrupted, but Kennedy gave me a nod.

"How do you know I've been meeting with the KGB?" I asked McCone.

McCone reached into his briefcase and threw a sheaf of 8 x 11 photos on to the table. The president picked up the top one, examined it, and held it up to me. There in black and white sat Volkov and I eating lunch.

"That other man with Mr. Michaels is Maxim Volkov, the station chief of the KGB," McCone said.

"Yes, they're at a restaurant," Kennedy said in a conversational voice. "The Occidental, isn't it?"

"I'm not necessarily saying he's a professional spy. His tradecraft is far from stellar." McCone had raised his voice as if that would help convey the import of what he was saying to the president.

"The Russians can be sloppy, can't they?"

McCone heard the president's sarcasm and folded his arms across his chest. He said, "Michaels' father had strong ties to the Communist Party."

"Excuse me, sir," I said to Kennedy. "Another question?" Another, less reluctant nod from him. I turned to McCone. "You have a guy about six feet tall who wears a fedora and a trench coat and sunglasses following me?"

McCone tightened the grip of his arms around his own ribcage.

"Answer him, please, John," Kennedy said.

McCone, though, addressed the response to his boss. "Yes, sir. He is, sir. What else could I do? Michaels was meeting with the KGB."

Bobby said, "John, keeping track of the KGB in this country is the FBI's job, right? By law?"

The president didn't give McCone the chance to answer his brother. He said, "Looks like your tradecraft isn't so great either, John, if an amateur like Nate here can spot a tail."

"If he really is an amateur."

"Oh, Nate's a spy, is he? And am I a spy too, if I've known Volkov since before the War?" Kennedy asked.

"No, sir."

Kennedy winced as he leaned forward. The situation with McCone or his back again? "John, the CIA works for you and you work for me. Mr. Michaels is working for me too. If you want to question any of my decisions, feel free, but do it to my face and not by sneaking around behind my back." Kennedy's eyes were narrowed and locked on McCone's. The others were all looking downward, seemingly overtaken by a simultaneous urge to check their shoeshines. "Got it?" Kennedy asked.

"Yes, sir," McCone said.

"May I say one more thing?" I asked.

"What?" Kennedy snapped.

I was pressing my luck, I knew. As he'd told me twenty-two years ago at that party with Lombard and Gable, the world situation belonged to him, not me. I turned to smile at McCone. "Tell the man in the trench coat thank you for saving my life."

"He violated instructions by interfering," the CIA director said.

"Then thank him for his initiative as well."

McCone gave me an abrupt nod, but Kennedy said, "It remains to be seen whether saving Mr. Michaels' life was in the country's best interests."

He laughed, and I joined in.

"One last question before we go to bed," Kennedy said. "Who's going to be in charge of a new civil government for Cuba after the invasion?"

I could hear air being exhaled around the table. The president had made his point and was ready to turn back to the business at hand. The others around the table had satisfied themselves as to the state of their footwear and looked up.

McNamara replied, "We have a task force working on it. We ought to take time tomorrow to talk about that."

Sorensen asked, "What time did we decide on meeting tomorrow morning?"

McNamara answered, "Eleven thirty."

The meeting was breaking up. Groups of two or three huddled and began talking among themselves.

I was sitting against the wall three feet behind the Defense Secretary. Bobby Kennedy leaned his way and asked, "How are you doing, Bob?"

"Well. How about yourself?" McNamara responded.

"All right."

"You got any doubts?"

"Well, no. I think we're doing the only thing we can do."

As McNamara said, "We need to have two things ready," the other groups quieted. "First, as the president said, a government for Cuba because we're going to need one after we invade, and secondly, plans for how to respond to the Soviet Union in Europe, because sure as hell they're going to do something there."

"We need to figure out what they might do," Douglas Dillon, the Treasury Secretary said.

"I'd suggest that it will be an eye for an eye," McNamara said.

McCone had been caught with his fingers in the cookie jar, but he wasn't pouting. He said, "I'd love to take Cuba away from Castro." He'd accomplish something his predecessor had failed to do at the Bay of Pigs.

Sorensen had the meeting's last word. "Suppose we make Bobby mayor of Havana?"

Bobby pushed his forelock back and smiled. His brother laughed again. I did too. Maybe a little too hard.

But why not laugh on Saturday? War was coming on Sunday.

Chapter Eighteen

The shadowy figure loomed in the doorway to my third-floor White House room as it had on the other nights.

"Sorry about that business with McCone downstairs," the president said and leaned against the doorframe.

"Well, like you said, it doesn't matter where you stand...."

"It matters where you sit," Kennedy finished.

"And the CIA's job is spying so they spy. That's the way it is."

"And they didn't want anyone else stepping on their turf," he said. "What's it been, three days? You're already an old Washington hand."

"I'll take that as the insult it was meant to be."

"Anyway, you figured out who the guy in the trench coat was."

"So what?" I said. "The Austrian-Hungarian Empire figured out who killed Archduke Ferdinand, and it didn't matter. World War I still came."

He sighed. "Come on downstairs. Dave and I are going to watch a movie."

"Let me call home and then I'll be right down."

"Don't you want to know what movie?" Jack asked.

"I don't much care." Watching any film would be a better way to kill time than lying awake and thinking of what was coming. Being with Kennedy and Powers would be better than lying on the bed counting off the hours until the world ended.

"Okay. Come find us in the theater."

He left and I picked up the phone. The operator put me through.

"Is that you, Dad?"

"Hi, Sam."

"No, it's Jake."

"It's seven thirty on a Saturday night. Why aren't you out?"

"We didn't want to miss your call so Cindy and Kathy came over here. They're with Mom in the kitchen making dessert."

"Put Sam on the other extension."

Their musical taste hadn't changed while I was gone. They'd turned down the stereo to answer the phone, but the soft wailing of "Twist and Shout" was still providing a soundtrack to our conversation. My wife liked the boys' music, the rock and roll, but I was still a Tommy Dorsey, Glenn Miller, Duke Ellington big band guy.

"Hey, Dad." It was hard to tell which twin I was talking to, but it had to be Sam. "Cindy wants to know if you've met Jackie." Sam, it was. His girlfriend was Cindy.

"Yeah, I have."

"Hey, Cin, Dad says he's met her." A high-pitched scream came through the handset, backed up by the stereo's imprecation to "shake it up, baby."

"Do you think you'll make it home by Thursday for the cross-country meet?"

"Gonna try. Boys, I've been thinking. When I get back, let's go car shopping."

No answer.

"You boys don't want a car?"

"Yeah, but you said not until we earned the money ourselves."

"I'll make it a loan. You'll pay me back."

"You said no to that before."

"I changed my mind."

One of the boys yelled out, "Mom, Dad says we can get a car."

The other shouted in his extension, "Thank you, Dad. Thank you."

"Calm down for a second, boys. I want you to remember that I love you both."

"Dad, are you going soft on us?"

"Yeah, I guess so."

One whispered "I love you too" was followed by another. They didn't want their girlfriends to hear them saying words to their old man that they probably hadn't said to them.

"Good night. Let me talk to Mom."

Her first words into the handset were, "Really, Nate? You said they could buy a car now?"

"A used one. Make sure they know it's a used one."

"After what they pulled yesterday, I don't know," she said.

"What did they do?"

"They cut school."

"You didn't tell me."

"Well, you have enough to worry about."

"What did they do?" I asked.

"They rode their bikes up to Searsville Lake."

"With the girls?"

"Sure. They said they were sick of the air raid drills."

No wonder they were surprised about the car. What the hell? If the world was going to end, why not spend a day lolling around the lake with their girlfriends?

"I'm playing hooky from work too, aren't I? Chalk it up to me setting a bad example. How angry are you at those nudniks of ours?" I asked.

"Well, if you're not mad at them, things must be pretty bad back there." She could read me.

"I think the boys had a good idea – time to get out of Palo Alto. Remember the hotel we stayed in on the beach in Mendocino the summer before last? Why don't you take a drive up there tonight?"

"They do have school Monday."

"I think the boys had the right idea. Being on the beach makes more sense than hiding under desks in Palo Alto. Just stay until I call." There were no military targets up there. And the extra couple hundred miles could push my family beyond range of the Soviet missiles in Cuba. Kennedy had sent Jackie and his kids to the country. I was following his example.

"Oh, my God. It is that bad."

Of course it was, but I said, "I hope not. Your idea to let the Russians think they were getting a win was terrific."

"It helped?"

"We'll see. Promise me you'll leave tonight."

"I'd rather come out to Washington and be with you."

"Promise," I demanded.

"I promise."

"It should only be a couple more days. Take care of the boys."

"This is different from a business trip," she said. "God, I miss you."

"I love you." I hadn't told her that in years.

I heard her breathing into the phone. "After everything we've been through? After all this time?" she asked. "Still?"

"More than ever. Good night. I'll see you and the boys soon."

"God willing," she responded.

After I hung up, I mulled over her last words. It's all God's will? Without human influence? At the beginning of the Book of Genesis, there's nothing, a complete void, until God says, "Let there be light." Then *poof*, there's light, the universe is called into being. Astronomers and physicists have put together a big bang theory that's pretty consistent with that biblical account. So if everything started with a huge explosion, would we come full circle and end that way too, with nuclear bombs destroying millions, billions, all life?

What difference did it make anyway? A million years ago humans were little more than the smartest of the apes. A million years from now we'd be looked on as benighted creatures ourselves. Any connection between these potential descendants and me seemed so attenuated as to be meaningless.

I whacked my palm against the side of my head. Enough with the mental gymnastics. Logic might say that what happened in the next twenty-four hours didn't matter in the long run, but in the short run, it mattered to me, mattered more than anything. We'd had our crises, but I did love my wife and was too selfish to want to give up the years I had left with her. Then there were our kids. Whatever happened eons from now, the twins hadn't had their full turn at life yet in this twentieth century. Why should they be deprived of it? There was always a chance they wouldn't screw things up like my generation had.

Someone once said a man without children has no future. I had two. I needed to protect my future.

Chapter Nineteen

I sneaked into a seat on one side of the president. A few seconds later Powers handed me a tub of popcorn. "We didn't wait for you," he said.

Up on the theater-sized screen shone Audrey Hepburn, whose slim elegance was so redolent of Jackie's. Was that why her husband had picked *Roman Holiday* to watch? Or was he trying to flee the world of Cold War, Cuba, and coercion for ninety minutes to take refuge in a fairy tale realm of romance and royalty?

If it were the latter, I was glad to join him in the dark, ensconced in a loge seat covered in crushed velvet. I'd finished with the popcorn before the princess had finished with the reporter in the movie.

The lights came on. We were back in the basement of the East Wing.

"She had to do her duty, didn't she?" Kennedy asked. "It's like O'Hara's *Appointment in Samarra*. You ever read that, Nate?"

"Sure. O'Hara's my man. You can't escape your destiny."

He snapped his fingers. "You recommended it to me, didn't you? During the War I saw a Seabee reading it. I asked if I could borrow it when he was done, but he just ripped it in two and handed me the first half which I read before going out on patrol that night. Only that was the night something else was ripped in half – my PT boat." He was looking down at the floor, not at me, and smiled at his own joke. "Anyway, I didn't get to read the second half until

I was in the hospital back in Boston. You know what I thought after I finished it? That under his skin Nate Michaels is an Irish Catholic fatalist, like me and John O'Hara."

Now he gave me an accusatory stare, but I'd already philosophized enough on my own before joining him and Powers.

"Can you order up whatever movie you want?" I asked.

He hesitated while deciding whether to go along with my change in direction. Then he said, "Yup. There are two great things about being president. The swimming pool and this …." He waved his hand around the miniature movie palace.

If there was anything else, I sure couldn't think of it right then. "Good choice of movies," I told him. "I haven't seen it since it came out."

"Bob Stack told me that Peck ad-libbed the scene where he put his hand in the stone lion's mouth. Hepburn's scream was for real. You remember Stack taking us to that Hollywood party?"

"Sure. You were talking to Clark Gable. You know, I saw him during the War. He remembered you."

"That's a surprise. He seemed pretty bored when we talked."

"I ran into him in the officer's mess at Chelveston in '43 or '44. He was a gunner with the 351st, but flew just a couple missions. The brass didn't want to take a chance on losing him – they figured it would be bad for morale back home. He was frustrated. He wanted to get back up there. He even asked if I could get him a transfer to the 305th so he could fly with me."

"You said no?"

"I went through the motions, but there was no way to pull it off. He was trying to get himself killed."

"Because his wife had died?"

"Yeah, I think so."

"Carole Lombard. What a beauty. Damn plane crashes kill too many people. Before coming down here, I had to write a letter to the widow of the U-2 pilot."

With that quick segue, we left Hollywood and fantasy land and returned to a world on the precipice.

Powers got up and came back a few seconds later with snifters half-filled with dusky amber liquid. I sipped the drink this time. Cognac, old and smooth.

"So what's going to happen?" Kennedy asked me.

"What happens now isn't up to us, is it?"

"Dave, what time is church tomorrow morning?" he asked.

"Ten."

Turning back to me, he said, "Nope, it's not all up to us,"

Powers left the theater. Kennedy and I talked about our kids. Five minutes later the door to the theater reopened and Powers came in, this time accompanied by a blonde. I stood up. Kennedy didn't.

"Thanks for coming by so late, Mary," he said. "Mary, meet my old friend from Stanford, Nate Michaels. Nate, Mrs. Meyer."

Mrs. Meyer held out her hand, palm down, just as Jackie had. I looked down at my buttery, salted fingers. "Um, I've been eating popcorn," I explained.

"They do over-butter it here, don't they? I'm used to it."

I squeezed her hand. She sat down in the loge where Powers had watched the movie. He moved to a seat in the second row.

"Mr. Michaels," she said. "I don't know how you can relax with a movie."

"Me? I don't know how the president does it," I said with a look over at Kennedy.

She shook her head. "Can you believe an hour after his speech announcing the quarantine Monday night, Jack and Jackie were hosting a dinner party for her sister and Oleg Cassini?"

"*Roman Holiday* really does provide an escape," I said.

"One of my favorites," she said and embarked on an oral tour of the Eternal City. She'd been everywhere from St. Peter's to the catacombs.

Mary Meyer was no bimbo. Her hair was cut short and her face wore the wrinkles around her eyes comfortably. She had at least a decade on Jackie, but still had a patrician style and Seven Sisters accent in common with her. Like Jackie, she would have looked at home on a yacht in Newport. President of the United States or not, Kennedy could still think of himself as an Irish parvenu. What he appreciated in Jackie – class – this woman had too. He wanted to get close to them and have some rub off.

"What does Benjy think?" Kennedy was saying. He turned to me. "Mrs. Meyer's brother-in-law is Ben Bradlee, the Washington correspondent for *Newsweek*."

The topic had turned back to Cuba during my ruminations. Kennedy seemed willing to discuss current events with this woman, if not his wife.

"My sister says he's so busy getting the magazine out that he doesn't have time to think."

I stood. "Nice to meet you, Mrs. Meyer," I said with a smile. "I have an early morning appointment. Dave, Mr. President. Thank you for inviting me down here. Seeing that movie again was fun."

As with all Kennedy's conquests, I liked Mrs. Meyer and felt the pull of her appeal. What made her and Vi and Jackie and Miriam go for him, I didn't know. Never would.

As the door swung closed behind me, I could hear the president and Powers begin singing "When Irish Eyes Are Smiling."

I'd got out before frat time. The movie had provided diversion enough for me, but not for Kennedy. This is what Jackie had meant when she burst into my room. She must know what happened when she was away from the White House.

For the second time that day, I thought how in handling men, in being able to put himself in the other guy's shoes, Jack Kennedy had grown over the last twenty-two years. In his public life, then, I had to admire him. But still, my accusation from two nights ago had just been proven true beyond a reasonable doubt. In his private life, he had not changed at all. And Kennedy's counter-charge was just as true. I couldn't move beyond what had happened back at Stanford. If he hadn't changed, why *should* he be forgiven?

Chapter Twenty

"Michaels!"

I'd turned a corner on the way back to my room and saw Curtis LeMay pacing in the White House's entrance hall. I stood at attention while the general swooped in for a sortie with me as the target. My right arm started to levitate out of habit, but with a supreme act of will, I pushed it back down. The days when I had to salute him were long gone.

"General," I said.

"What are you doing here?" He didn't sound as though he were asking.

"The president asked me to come out from the Coast and lend a hand," I said.

He pushed his index finger into my sternum – not for the first time. His beefy face loomed inches from mine with a dead cigar held between his teeth. Its gnawed end dripped tobacco juice over my suit jacket.

I'd transferred from the Royal Canadian Air Force into the newly constituted American Eighth Bomber Command in the spring of 1942. LeMay, then a lieutenant colonel, had taken over my unit, the 305th Bomber Group, that fall. "I hear you went to law school" were his first words to me and in saying them, he'd put his finger against my chest for the first time. "Yes, sir," I told him. "I don't like lawyers," he'd said to me. "They're talkers, not doers."

"The president? He chickened out again," LeMay was saying. "How in hell do you get men to risk their lives when the SAMs are not attacked? I need to speak to him."

"Why? It's twelve forty in the morning."

"I had standing orders to fire on any SAM site that fired on us. I was getting ready to let them have it when . . ." He held out a piece of note paper.

I read aloud. "'Do not launch attack on SAM sites without direct authorization from CinC.'" The note was signed "McNamara."

"McNamara, smart? Yes. But a leader, no."

"He ran Ford," I said.

"I've known him since '45 when he was an Army Air Forces statistician. He was superb at *that* job. Now he's chickened out. He's letting the White House push us around."

The tables had turned. Now LeMay worked for McNamara. And McNamara was showing more loyalty to the president than to the Air Force.

The general stopped pushing against my chest and took a step back. "How long you known Kennedy?"

"Since before the War," I answered.

"You live out in California?"

"Yeah."

"I lived in Emeryville when I was a kid." LeMay's tone was wistful.

"That's across the Bay from us."

"One of my planes brought you back here?" Now he was back to business.

"That's right."

"So can you get me into see Kennedy?" the general asked.

As if this were a logical quid pro quo for the flight across the country . . . .

"Now?"

"Now," he said.

Sure, I'd interrupt the president if it would do any good – the fate of the country counted for more than singing old Irish tunes. But it wouldn't. He'd made a decision not to retaliate this weekend unless the reconnaissance planes were fired on tomorrow. No wait, it was after midnight. Later today.

"No."

"When I got Taylor on the phone, he said the same thing." He chomped down on the cigar and sprayed a little more tobacco juice on my jacket. "When will you see him next?"

"The president?" I asked.

"Who the hell else?"

"Tomorrow morning."

"Come with me," he said.

"Why?"

"Because I'm not going to bed and you're here and no one else will listen to any sense."

Before LeMay took over the 305th, we'd take evasive action to avoid German flak and straighten out over the target for ten seconds. That didn't give us time to drop our bombs accurately. At our briefing on November 23, 1942, the first one under his command, LeMay told the crews we would approach the German sub pens at St. Nazaire straight as a ruler. Over the howling, LeMay said, "If any of you don't have the stomach for this, see the adjutant for a transfer." No day that starts at 0300 is a good day, I remember thinking. The room quieted when LeMay said he would be leading the run himself. The 305th didn't lose a single plane that day, even though for seven minutes before reaching the pens, we took no evasive action. We put twice as many bombs on the target as any other group. Old Iron Ass was the War's genius of aerial bombing.

"Let's go, Michaels," he said.

I hadn't figured on being able to sleep anyway. It was better to listen to LeMay than let him fuss and fume. Besides, I owed him. He had put me in harm's way during the War, but had led me through it too. And one more thing: unlike anyone else involved in this crisis, he'd given the order twice already. Enola Gay and Bockscar, the B-29s that dropped the atomic bombs on Hiroshima and Nagasaki in 1945, had been under his command.

"Yes, sir," I replied.

Chapter Twenty-One

By the time the Cadillac limousine with a four-star flag waving from the hood pulled into the Pentagon garage, I was more than ready to try to escape. Torture of prisoners was prohibited by the Geneva Convention, but LeMay's relit cigar stump had my eyes stinging and my throat raw. It might be a little after one in the morning, but an Air Force major was there to swing the car door open for the general. He stifled a cough as the miasma hit his face.

On the elevator LeMay poked me again with his index finger while his other four fingers formed a fist that clutched the cigar.

"Okay, son, you pay attention to me. We are ready. The sooner we move the better." He was only about ten years older than I was, but given my bomber pedigree, he was ready to add paternal pressure to his argument.

The elevator spit us out into a hallway. After a couple dozen paces clicking on linoleum, LeMay tugged a door open and we entered a room thrumming with jangling phones, clacking teletypes, and *sotto voce* consultations. Behind a long curving table sat fifteen airmen who stared at the wall in front of them where swooping second hands rotated across green radar screens. On the far wall were thumbtacked dozens of photographs. I moved closer to see how they compared to what I'd seen at the NPIC. Yes, some of Soviet soccer fields and camouflaged missiles, but even more of sandy beaches, where soldiers and marines could be landing in little more than thirty-six hours.

LeMay, hands on his hips, was admiring a huge world map that covered the left wall. It was dotted with hundreds of push pins, predominantly red, with some white sprinkled through the continental United States and blue in the Pacific and Atlantic Oceans. He stuck his cigar butt back in his mouth and held out his hand. A pointer was slapped into it with a crack. "Listen up," he ordered.

It didn't matter that the audience consisted only of me. He'd done countless briefings for pilots during the War before they took off to drop a load on occupied France, Nazi Germany, or Imperial Japan, and he must have figured I'd listened to my share by the very fact that I'd been a bomber pilot and was still alive. In those briefings my job had been to absorb information on my target and enemy defenses, not to question the wisdom or purpose of the mission. LeMay wanted to get me in the right frame of mind.

I leaned back against the curved table, paying life-or-death attention to what I was being told as though it were indeed twenty years ago.

"The whole Strategic Air Command is on nuclear alert," LeMay said.

"These white pins are nuclear-armed bombers. There's 1,600 of them." He pointed at air bases around the country and in Europe. "These B-52s are in the air now." He pointed at pins hovering over Alaska, Canada, Florida, England, West Germany, and the Arctic Ocean.

He waved his stick over North Dakota and moved it toward California. "These are ICBMs, 177 waiting for the word." He stopped. "You say something?"

I hadn't, but now said, "Remarkable."

"You bet your ass," he responded. "We got all the firepower we need to do the job."

But that's not what I'd been thinking. LeMay had started his career in the age of open cockpit biplanes and now was presiding over a flock of intercontinental missiles. Remarkable.

"Right," I told him. They say masters start looking like their dogs. With his cylindrical bulk narrowing at the neck and head, LeMay, master of the Strategic Air Command, resembled nothing more than one of his pet missiles.

He waved at the blue dots in the oceans. "Now these are Navy submarines." He shrugged. His voice and body language indicated both skepticism – about whether the Polaris missiles would even work – and magnanimity – in mentioning nuclear weapons not in his bailiwick. He just plumb didn't like the Navy. Maybe LeMay's disdain for the president stemmed from Kennedy's naval heritage.

I listened to the general talk about the five Looking Glass command planes out of Offut Air Force Base in Nebraska, one of which was always in the air.

He took his pointer up to the photographs on the wall. I watched it flit from reconnaissance shot to reconnaissance shot. "Look here. Every day, every hour, the Russians have more of their missiles go fully operational. The sooner we move the better. Moving now will save American lives." LeMay hit the pointer against his palm. "Any questions?" he barked.

"The Jupiters in Turkey aren't on the map," I said.

"Those pieces of crap? Why should they be? They're useless. We don't need them to be ready to go. We're ready to go without them."

"I'm sure the president will be glad to hear that. I understand the Russians have battlefield nukes in Cuba, don't they?"

He squinted at me a second before nodding. "Once my pilots finish with Cuba, it will be a walk-in." He hit the pointer against his palm again. "A walk-in. This is what we've been waiting for. Goddammit, wouldn't you like to climb into one of those bombers yourself and let them have it?"

Was the "them" the Russians in Cuba or the Russians in Russia? Didn't matter. "My days in the cockpit are long gone. Better leave this to those who've been training for it," I said.

I wasn't sure he heard me. "Goddammit, *I* would," he muttered. Then he looked up. "Backing down now would be the worst defeat in American history."

Once war came, this country would be lucky to have LeMay as commander of its air force. But until then, he was a bull tethered in the ring, straining at the ropes.

Chapter Twenty-Two

I'm not a regular coffee drinker and that's why the muddy, bitter brew I'd slurped down at the Pentagon had such an effect on me. On the ride back to the White House, my fingertips jittered against my thighs and my eyelids twitched every couple seconds. The lack of sleep didn't help either. Nor did the pending cremation of thousands, maybe millions, maybe all mankind.

The White House switchboard was on duty twenty-four hours a day. I had them put me through to home. No answer even after 20 rings. Good, the family had left already. Had it been fair to warn my family? Why not? Jack had. Wait, I wasn't going to use him as my moral exemplar, not in family matters. The thought that anyone could read the papers and see the danger calmed my roiling conscience somewhat little.

When the mess opened at six thirty, I was there. Alone. I leafed through the Sunday *New York Times*. I stopped as I read the oversized type of a headline: "Will There be War? The Question the World Is Asking."

With each word of the article, more of my appetite went AWOL. Still, I stuffed a cheese omelet and two pieces of toast slathered with butter and jam down my gullet. Whether hungry or not, I had eaten like that before a mission during the War too. Not *right* before or I'd throw it up, but with three or four hours to go. I needed the strength and who knew when I'd have another chance to eat?

Jack was going to church this morning, presumably to pray. That wasn't going to work for me. What could I do? I was drumming my fingers on the table and asking the Filipino steward for more coffee when McNamara came into the room. His eyebrows went up as he saw me. He'd figured on being alone this early on a Sunday morning, just as I had.

"Join me, Bob?"

He sat down and ordered steak and eggs. To be companionable I asked for a bowl of oatmeal.

"Ah." McNamara took his first sip of coffee. Unlike me, he had taken care of his grooming before breakfast. He'd shaved closely enough that his cheeks glowed in the overhead lights. As always, his hair was swept back with Brylcreem. His white shirt was so heavily starched, it crackled as he moved. The perfection of his blue tie's Windsor knot belonged on a mannequin in the window of Brooks Brothers.

"Looks like you're all ready...." I said.

He peered at me over the rim of the cup, through his wire-rims.

"General LeMay took me through the preparations last night," I explained. "Or rather this morning. You've known him for a long time?"

"Sure have. He might be the best wartime leader we've ever produced."

"But it's not wartime yet," I said.

He shook his head. "Not to you or me. But LeMay figures it's inevitable, and if we are going to fight, it would be a waste not to use thermonuclear weapons."

"But he wouldn't act on his own?"

"No, never. He didn't become the youngest four-star general since Grant by being a fool. He knows how to follow orders. He also knows how to voice his opinion."

"So I noticed."

"He's lobbying to take out the missile installations," McNamara said.

"He should get his chance soon."

"He doesn't want to wait. We're going to send the recon flights over the Russian missile installations in a few hours. They'll either fire at our planes or not. If they do, we'll take out their SAM sites like LeMay wants."

"Like that." I snapped my fingers.

"It's a decision tree. We've gone through each step."

IBM had big computers with flashing lights and big spools of magnetic tape. Cutting open McNamara's skull would doubtless reveal a miniaturized version of the same. Kennedy had what he needed in his defense secretary – a logic engine. You didn't want to have someone like me, who might let emotions enter the equation, anywhere near the planning function for World War III.

"And you're going to take the president through that tree this morning?"

"I came over here just in case."

Had LeMay bullied him into it? Maybe. But it didn't matter. Kennedy wasn't going to see him without the rest of the members of the ExComm. From what I'd seen, he wasn't meeting one-on-one with anyone except Bobby, Dave Powers, and me. Oh yeah, and Mrs. Meyer. After what he'd been up to last night, he'd sleep late. He'd take his swim and then head over to church before ten. Just a normal lazy Sunday morning. Like the one on December 7, 1941.

Kennedy had guts, that's for sure. And McNamara? He was nervous in the service – he didn't want to sit around the Pentagon waiting.

"When will our planes begin their overflights?" I asked.

"They'll take off before noon."

I looked at my watch. "Less than five hours. If they're fired on, when will we move?"

"Well, we'll want to get the photos back from the planes – the ones that make it back – for targeting. By three."

"You have a family, Bob?"

He started. "Yeah. Margaret and I were sweethearts at Cal ...."

"Hey, I went to Cal too," I said. "Class of '39."

"Class of '37 for me. Margaret and I got married three years later. We have two girls and a boy." Of all things, Bob McNamara, former Harvard Business School professor, former president of Ford Motor Company, wiped away a tear.

Shit. There was a real person behind those glasses, and I'd stumbled upon him. Damn. I'd thrown the sand of his personal life into the computerized gears of his mind.

"Beat Stanford," I said as I got up.

"Right. Big Game is supposed to be in three weeks," he replied.

"Let's hope so."

"Beat Stanford," he said.

"Good luck with the briefing."

He tried to smile, and I headed back up to my room.

Chapter Twenty-Three

I was lying on my bed, looking at my watch every couple of minutes. In between time checks, I wondered if Kennedy had started his swim yet. For me a nap was out of the question. Not with all that caffeine racing through my bloodstream. Not with only a few hours until Navy F-4 Crusaders started snapping their photos of the Soviet missile sites.

What could I do? I'd told Volkov what would happen if the planes were fired on. To make sure the message got through, Kennedy had had Bobby warn Dobrynin too. Each step was pre-determined. We'd made a decision tree. Presumably, Khrushchev and company had done the same. Any action would be met by a fixed response. The dominoes would fall – *click, click.* We would march in lockstep through the gates of hell.

Then, what I'd done to McNamara, I did to myself. He hadn't wanted to go back to those days before the War with his college sweetheart and neither did I, but with another war on the way, that's where we both ended up.

The Army Air Forces didn't count the missions I'd flown for the RAF toward its limit of thirty-five. Of the original 160 flyers in the 508th squadron, only seventeen made it that far. Many had been killed by flak, German fighters, or mechanical malfunction, but not most. A couple of dozen hit the limit, a small number were seriously wounded, some transferred, a few waited for war's end in some German stalag, a single crew acquired a taste for aquavit while interned in neutral Sweden. But so many of those who didn't make it had better reasons to live than I did. Our crew didn't fly as often as others in the summer of 1944, because we flew lead, a more dangerous assignment. Still, by October of that year, I hit the limit with a bombing raid on a bridge across the Rhine at Cologne. Something had gone wrong – Death had forgotten to come for me – and I was ordered to take home leave.

So I headed back to the States to see my family. I was lucky to catch a Dakota at the base in Old Buckenham that stopped in Scotland, Iceland, and Labrador as it skipped its way across the Atlantic. Flying across the country from Presque Island, Maine, was a tougher challenge. It took a week of waiting in air terminals before I could cadge the four rides that ended at Hamilton Field on San Pablo Bay, north of San Francisco.

I didn't know how she found out about my arrival, but it must have been from my parents – I'd sent them a Western Union from San Antonio. Over the last three years she'd written dozens of letters on V-Mail's blue tissue paper. Sometimes I'd hold on to one for a couple of days, maybe even holding it up to the light to try to read it, but in the end I'd send it back unopened, like all the others.

I wasn't looking for any reception committee when I tossed my duffel down on the tarmac, nor when I held on to the bar at the bottom of the hatch to swing myself down from the plane. But when my feet hit the ground, I looked up and there she was, wearing a WAAF uniform, thirty feet away. I stared. Her cap floated on a cloud of golden hair. The October sun glinted off her blue eyes. The sergeant's stripes on her shoulders must have enabled her to follow my progress across the country. I stood paralyzed as she ran the dozen steps to me and grabbed my upper arms hard, hard so I wouldn't flee.

Miriam looked up at me and said, "I'm sorry. I was wrong." Her eyes were moist, her gaze direct. She shook me. "Don't you understand? I did not love him. It's you I love."

For a moment, two seconds or maybe five, what she said made everything worthwhile – the nightmares, the missions, the shell fragments in my leg. Her words were what I'd wished for, her face the one that had haunted me since Stanford. I shook my head to dispel the dream and then shook loose my arms, picked the duffel back up, and started walking toward the terminal. I couldn't help it – in my mind's eye I was seeing her again through the window in Kennedy's cottage. She might have called my name, but I didn't turn around.

What an idiot.

⌣

I reached for the phone and had the White House operator ring the hotel in Mendocino.

"Hello, dear," I said.

"What time is it?" Sleep slurred her voice.

"Four thirty your time."

"Anything wrong?" She was wide awake.

"No, I just wanted to hear your voice."

"Are you coming back to us soon?"

"Soon. Tell the boys I love them. You too."

"You be careful."

The operator interrupted, "Mr. Michaels, a Mr. Volkov would like to talk to you."

"Gotta take this, dear."

"Be careful," she said again. I heard the click when she hung up. "Put him through," I told the operator.

I wiped my eyes on the pillow.

Chapter Twenty-Four

"Nathan Solomonovich, you've got to stop all planes," Volkov said.

Nathan, son of Solomon. He was invoking my father's memory as if he'd been a Catholic saint who could perform miracles. Funny thing for an atheist to try when speaking to a Jew.

"Why are you calling?"

"You need to stop overflights. Khrushchev did not give order to shoot American U-2 yesterday."

"He does not have control over the military in Cuba?"

"There was communications problem."

"It's me, Maxim. Just give me a straight answer."

"No, he does not."

And Volkov had been worried about Kennedy's control over our generals.

"If there is an overflight today, the planes will be shot at?"

"Yes," Volkov said.

"I don't think I can stop the overflights based on what you're telling me."

"*Derr'mo*," he cursed. "American generals want own planes shot down? So they have excuse for war."

He had LeMay pegged. Neither of us spoke for half a minute. Then he continued, "When first American lands on Cuban beach, Red Army enters West Berlin."

I closed my eyes and watched the events unroll in the newsreel of my mind. Overflight, anti-aircraft missiles, bombing the sites, invasion of Cuba. The uncrossable line would be crossed. The local Russian generals would use their tactical nuclear weapons rather than suffer a defeat in Cuba. Our generals would use their nukes rather than suffer defeat in Germany.

A single human life goes through stages – conception, gestation, birth, infancy, youth, prime, old age. If the entire human race had been conceived in the Garden of Eden, perhaps today, October 28, 1962, its death rattles would begin.

I had the sense that Volkov knew what was running through my head. "It is your generals who want war," I said.

"They are willing to fight war to avoid defeat. Unless victory without war, war will come."

LeMay had said almost the same thing. It's just that Russian generals weren't quite so committed to civilian control.

"Let's meet face-to-face," I said into the handset.

"For what?" he asked.

Volkov didn't know we had a few hours before the overflights began.

"We need to figure out how to give your countrymen a victory," I told him. "Where are you?"

Chapter Twenty-Five

The Secret Service hadn't interfered when I went off in LeMay's Air Force car eight hours ago, but the two agents standing in front of the White House door had been instructed not to let me out on my own.

A few minutes later then I was in the back seat of a gray government Chevrolet on the way to 1448 Swann Street in the District. I'd told the agents I had a meeting there, but neglected to mention that we were on our way to a safe house to visit the head of the KGB in North America.

Negro families in their Sunday best were parading down Swann toward St. James Apostle Church on the corner of Fifteenth. Both sides of the street were lined by cars. More churchgoers. Our Chevy crunched its way over those spiky balls gingko trees dropped in the fall. The driver stopped in front of a lemon custard-colored row house. His partner followed me up the steps to a wrought iron platform at front-door level, hand inside suit jacket poised over shoulder holster. I rang the doorbell.

We were being examined through a fish-eye lens. The door opened a crack and a right hand with lacquered red nails grabbed my arm.

I peeked around the door. "Hello, Miss Leontieva." The red nails on her left hand were wrapped around the gleaming hardness of an automatic. So I was standing between an armed and ready

KGB agent in front of me and Secret Service agents behind me. I knew they were on the same side, but they might not.

Volkov waddled into the front hallway and spread his arms wide. "Nathan," he bellowed.

I turned back to the agent. "All's fine."

"Only you," Miss Leontieva said.

I turned to look at the agent who shook his head.

"They've got to come in too," I said.

She turned to Volkov, who dropped his chin an inch.

One of the agents brushed by me and confronted Leontieva. She tucked her gun into the waistband of her skirt. He ran up the stairs. A minute later he came down and declared, "These are the only two here."

Leontieva pointed at the bag I held in my hand. "What do you have?"

She watched me extract the cordovan shoes Volkov had loaned me. They dropped to the floor when Volkov wrapped his arms around me.

"Thanks, Maxim," I said when he released me from the bear-hug. "I don't know how I would have explained a missing shoe when I got back to the White House."

Volkov and I left his cordovans on the floor and the gunslingers in the kitchen and climbed up the stairs ourselves. I followed Volkov into a small room, once perhaps a bedroom for a live-in maid. He flicked a switch that turned on a red overhead bulb. In the ruddy gloaming I could make out two windows covered by black-out curtains. Volkov moved across the room and raised them. Now I could see shallow pans of liquid shimmering on a long table against the left-hand wall of the room. Above them was a cork bulletin board with push pins. We were in a darkroom, but in my honor any photos had been removed. On the opposite wall squatted an oak desk. Its roll top was open and revealed what looked like a boxy radio and clunky teletype machine.

Straight ahead between the windows stretched an army cot. Volkov gestured to the end of the bed and I sat up by the pillow and he at its foot. A thin brown wool blanket was pulled so tightly across the mattress that it could have been made only by a veteran enlisted man. I felt a lump under the pillow and pulled out a filmy black nightgown.

"Sorry. This must be where Miss Leontieva sleeps."

"Last night, yes. She listened for messages."

I stuffed the nightie back where I'd found it. The worker's state drabness that Miss Leontieva showed the world appeared to be only a shell.

"A real spy's lair, Maxim," I said, "but don't a few pasty-skinned Russians stick out in a Negro neighborhood?"

"I am where I belong, with proletariat." He smiled from his end of the bed, hands folded over his belly, feet widely spaced on the floor. "You say we stick out? No matter. We are not hiding from FBI."

"But you are hiding from the GRU."

"Hiding? No. KGB does not hide. We are being cautious."

"And the KGB does allow being cautious. You are staying away from the Embassy?"

"GRU agents there."

"But Miss Leontieva knows where you are and has been at the embassy too."

"GRU head in Washington believes in loyalty of Miss Leontieva." He pointed to the lump in the bed made by the nightie.

"I guess that approach to the GRU would not work quite as well for you, huh, Maxim?"

His laughter caused a bedquake. After it subsided, he said, "Better to have her sleeping with GRU head and working for me than other way 'round. I can trust her."

"The president's brother spoke to Ambassador Dobrynin last night. Which side is *he* on, yours or the GRU's?"

"Dobrynin will only call heads or tails after *grívennik* hits floor."

"The what?" I asked.

"Russian coin. Dobrynin will tell Nikita Sergeyevich he is loyal. He will whisper to generals what they want to hear."

"And they want to hear that it is time to confront the Americans?" I asked.

"*Da,*" Volkov said. "That man . . . ." He shook his head. "If he were not diplomat, he could be Moscow weatherman. Always he knows which way wind will blow. In twenty years when I am dead or retired in *dacha*, Dobrynin will still be living in embassy on Sixteenth Street. He will be friends with Kremlin *and* White House."

"Do you think he relayed the Attorney General's message back to Moscow?"

"It does not matter since I transmitted your message directly."

"How can you be sure *your* message got through?"

"Because I transmitted it from here." He pointed to the radio set on the desk. "I told Nikita Sergeyevich of president's promise not to invade Cuba. He was pleased. But he asked for more. Military want Americans to remove troops from Berlin. But Nikita Sergeyevich will accept American missiles out of Turkey."

"Right. I told you we were planning to take the missiles out of there anyway. The attorney general said the same thing to Dobrynin."

"That was mistake."

"Why? I told you the same thing."

"But Dobrynin's report will be circulated in Presidium. Soviet generals will feel deprived of triumph in protecting Motherland. Americans will say they have won."

"But if we don't say it, our generals will say we lost." I leaned toward the middle of the bed. "This is ridiculous. Is military pride enough to go to war over, for millions to die over?"

He shrugged. "The British went to war over ear of man called Jenkins."

"Back when they had iron cannons, not nuclear missiles," I said. "We will promise not to invade. You will withdraw your military missiles and bombers. And we will remove our missiles from Turkey in a few months. No crowing. President Kennedy will promise not to crow."

"Your president will not declare victory?"

"He will not."

"You can deliver this?"

"Yes," I said. I think I said it convincingly, but the folds of fat above and below Volkov's eyes squeezed together.

"Perhaps then you can deliver withdrawal of American troops from Berlin too?" he asked.

"Sure. And while we're at it, we could appoint Bertrand Russell Defense Secretary and give up all our nuclear weapons." I hit the bed with my hand. It responded with a satisfying twang. "We have our generals too. Even if you withdraw from Cuba, *our* generals will want to bomb anyway. They will view it as a defeat, an opportunity missed."

"Yes, I see." This made sense to him. He figured our generals would work like theirs. And of course he was right. It matters where you sit.

Like an Indian elephant rising from its knees, Volkov got up from the bed, took two paces over to the desk, and then sat on a rolling chair with three wheels. He put on earphones connected to what I still took to be a radio set. He took a pad of paper out of a drawer, pulled off a flimsy sheet covered with Cyrillic writing, and hammered something out on a crude keyboard between frequent glances back down at the pad.

After fifteen minutes, he took off the headphones and swiveled his chair around to face me. With a magician's flair, he pulled two eight-inch-long silver cylinders from an inside jacket pocket. "Would you like smoke while we wait?"

"I'm not ready to celebrate yet."

"For me it is practical matter. I will enjoy it now. I doubt Señor Castro will supply his socialist brothers with Montecristos if missiles removed. If missiles not removed, no more Señor Castro."

Impeccable logic.

While he started in that prolonged ritual of the cigar devotee, I asked, "Where is your message going?"

He lopped off the cigar's end. "One person who can decode sits in office next to Nikita Sergeyevich."

I looked down at my watch. Nine thirty. The overflights of Cuba were a couple of hours away. "What time is it in Moscow?" I asked.

He was running the long match up and down the cigar. "About six in evening."

I nodded.

He inhaled on the end of the cigar and the flame at the end of the match danced toward him. "We wait," he said. "Here in United States, hero of European War became president."

He was puffing away.

"Sure. Eisenhower served two terms."

"We have our own hero of European war."

"General Zhukov, but he was dismissed by Khrushchev."

"In 1957," he said.

"Ah. He'd be a popular replacement for Khrushchev if there is no victory in this Cuban matter." Just what we'd need. A military dictatorship in Moscow.

"Are your boys as smart as their father?" Volkov asked.

"Far smarter. They take after their mother. Khrushchev will not last long if he withdraws the missiles?"

"Between us, old friends? No more than two years."

"Even if we withdraw our missiles from Turkey?"

"No more than two years," he repeated.

For the next twenty minutes, between draws on his Montecristo, Volkov asked more about my family and reminisced about prewar San Francisco.

I jumped off the end of the bed with the first beep from the radio.

I was hovering over him as Volkov put the headphones back on and began scribbling. When he took the headphones off, I asked, "Good news?"

He shrugged and waved the paper in my face. Looked like it contained a couple of hundred characters.

He began translating what he'd written using a key on the top sheet of a pad of flimsies. He muttered to himself in Russian after every few scribbles. As he approached the end of the message, he started puffing harder on the cigar. Finally, he laid down the pencil and I saw his smile through a foggy haze. He stood, reached in his pocket, and pulled out another metal tube.

"Now you can have cigar," he said.

As he leaned over to hand me a celebratory smoke, his melon-shaped head exploded.

Chapter Twenty-Six

I dropped to the floor, bone fragments, brain, and blood splattered across my pants and shirt. I'd heard no firing before Volkov was hit, only the shattering of glass, but now the blast of gunfire concussed the room.

Leontieva rushed in. A muscle under her right eye quivered as she looked down at Volkov.

I stood and stepped over his body. I looked back. From this side, his head wound, massive as it was, couldn't be seen. Volkov's open eye had a distant look as if he were planning the next stratagem in the international chess game he'd been playing for three decades.

"We must go now," Leontieva said, dragging me by the sleeve.

"I can't leave the agents down there."

"Both dead. Come. The GRU will be in the house soon."

"Out the back?"

"No. They will have that covered." She pointed with the barrel of her gun. "We go up."

Right above me, set in the ceiling, was a door that must lead to an attic. If Volkov had been wrong about which side Leontieva was on, I'd be as dead as he was.

She was going over to the desk to get a chair.

The gunshots stopped.

I leapt up and pulled down on the handle. A collapsible wooden ladder unfolded to the floor.

"Good," she nodded with approval. "You go."

"Wait." I went over to Volkov and tugged on the piece of paper clutched in his hand. It started to tear. I knelt beside the body of my father's friend and uncurled his fingers one by one. I stuffed the paper into my pants pocket. Then I pushed his eyelid down with my index finger, yanked the blanket off the cot, and laid it over him.

Shaking her head as if to say "sentimental capitalist fool," Leontieva scampered up the ladder, her right hand on its side rail, the left grasping her gun. I followed and pulled the ladder and then the door up behind me. A crazy thought popped into my head – I was glad Volkov had managed that one last cigar.

As the door closed, the clanging of metal on metal began.

"The doors are reinforced steel." Leontieva said from a crouch as she straightened. She knocked aside a locking bar from a hatch above and pushed it open. A shaft of light hit me in the face.

Squinting, I gave her a boost and then went after her onto the roof of 1448 Swann. The banging was coming from the back door of the house. I heard the whine of approaching sirens. Thank God. One of those responsible churchgoers had called for help.

The banging stopped.

"The GRU is getting away," I said.

"No, they are in the house now," she said and put the hatch back over the opening. She kicked off her high heels. "Come."

She took short fast steps, her stride constricted by a tight black skirt. Like two cat thieves, we moved to the next roof and then the next.

We'd made it one more roof toward Fourteenth Street when a tremendous roar erupted behind us. I put my palms over my ears and turned to watch the hatch of 1448 Swann Street pop upward like an oversized champagne cork. A tan bubbly liquid did not follow, but yellow and red flames did.

"Grenades," Leontieva said. "*Now* you can be assured the GRU has left the house."

She reached down to grab the bottom of her skirt. Even over the noise from three doors down, I could hear the whooshing sound her skirt had made rubbing against her nylons. She started tugging.

"Let me." I ripped out the seams on either side of the skirt up to her garters at mid-thigh.

"Where is safe?" she asked.

Here we were in the capital of the Free World and the GRU had just missed killing us with gunfire and grenades. Another arm of the Soviet military might succeed soon enough with nuclear-tipped missiles launched from Cuba. No place in this fucking world was safe, was it? I looked down at my watch. Five after ten. Jack would be in church praying his heart out. I needed to get to him. Now.

"Come with me," I said to Leontieva.

With her skirt waving around the moving marble of her calves, Leontieva ran, her strides now matching mine as we moved over the tin and asphalt roofs of two dozen houses. We came to the last one before Fourteenth Street. A hatch to the attic formed a little broad-brimmed hat in the middle of the roof. I pulled. Locked.

I peered over the front edge of the roof at late churchgoers scurrying along Swann Street's sidewalks. It was a twenty-five-foot drop to a wrought iron platform by the house's front door. I'd been taught during the War how to roll when parachuting to the ground. Here there was no room to roll – the chances were better than even that one or both of us would break a leg. I moved along the perimeter of the roof to the Fourteenth Street side. An alley, about fifteen feet wide, separated us from the top of a store about ten feet lower down.

"With a running start we can make it there."

She came over and looked.

"I don't know," she said. "I'd rather go down in front."

"You'll break an ankle." I said. "We'll jump across together."

We walked back across the roof to get a running start of maybe twenty feet.

I stared at the opposite side of the roof we were on. We'd have to start our leap before the edge to clear the raised perimeter. I took a deep breath. Leontieva's skirt was flapping and snapping like a ship's ensign on a windy day. Then came a hiss and a whistle. I turned around to see two men about a dozen houses behind us, both holding guns that kicked up with each pull of the trigger. Leontieva whirled, knelt, and returned the fire. I lay down and peered over the roof edge. Handguns weren't much good at a distance of a hundred yards. Still, the men stopped and took cover behind a chimney.

She emptied her clip, stood, and dropped the gun with a clatter.

I bounced up and shouted, "Let's go." I grabbed her hand and we sprinted across the metal and asphalt of the roof and leapt into the void.

Chapter Twenty-Seven

I made it onto the store roof with a foot to spare, but Leontieva's jump carried her two feet less. I still had her by the hand, even after she hit the side of the building. I yanked and tried to fall forward. She yelled something in Russian, and I felt her grip loosen. I tightened my own.

Her weight was dragging me backward toward the edge of the roof.

"Let me go," she shouted. It was only ten feet from the soles of her feet to the ground. She'd live until the GRU assassins caught up with her.

"I'm going to pull." I yanked again. The tendons in my shoulder strained. She threw her free hand over the ridge on the side of the roof, and pulled herself up like a mountaineer.

We lay side by side, swallowing air.

We were, what, half a minute ahead of the gunmen?

"Come," I pulled on her arm.

She shrieked in pain.

"Get up," I yelled. "Get up or we die."

She made it to all fours and looked at me.

"Come on."

The pain pulled her lips back over her teeth to form a lioness's grin.

I grabbed her uninjured arm and dragged her to the edge of the building on Fourteenth Street. The sidewalk below was empty. Was everyone in church or had the gunfire caused any passersby to get the hell out of the way?

"You go," I said and grabbed both her arms to lower her. This time, even though she must have ripped tendons in one shoulder, no sound came from her throat beyond a quiet growl. Her feet dangled six feet above the sidewalk. A cat, she landed on her feet. I lowered myself and let go. I stumbled to one knee.

Looking back over my shoulder at the storefront, I could see we'd jumped off the roof of Wing's 14th Street Laundry and Cleaners.

At the corner of Swann, a couple dressed for church were getting out of a Yellow Cab. I shouted and waved. We ran and dove into the back seat just as the woman in a dress of ruffled pink with a matching hat got out.

"What were you doing up there on the roof?" the driver in his khaki uniform hat asked as I slammed the door.

I reached in my back pocket for my wallet and extracted a twenty. I held it up.

"Never mind that. Just get us to Saint Stephen Martyr Church," I said. "PDQ."

"On Pennsylvania between Twenty-fourth and Twenty-fifth?" he asked.

I didn't know my way around Washington at all. I looked at Leontieva.

She jerked her head forward. "*Da*. Yes. That's it."

"I don't know if you'll make it in time for Mass," the cabby said and put his foot down on the accelerator.

Chapter Twenty-Eight

I sat in the back seat behind the driver and turned my head toward Leontieva.

She tilted her head to acknowledge she had my attention and asked, "You fought in the War?"

"I did."

She nodded as though that explained something. I wasn't sure what relevance my war experience had. I'd discovered I'd rather face two Focke-Wulf 190s firing cannons at 19,000 feet than two GRU assassins firing handguns from a fifteen-foot-high rooftop.

"Maxim was a good man," I said.

"GRU pigs," she spat.

As if referring to them invoked their presence, the back window of the cab shattered.

I pushed Leontieva down.

The driver turned around either to look back at us or at the hole where a window had been a second before. I never found out which. He asked, "What was that?" and in reply a red crater the size of a quarter erupted right between his eyebrows.

The car was careening down New Hampshire Avenue at thirty-five miles an hour. When I leaned over to the front and squeezed the cabby's body down, he continued to clutch the steering wheel with a dead man's desperate grasp. The taxi hit a pothole and I slammed up against the upholstered ceiling and then was jackknifed against the top of the seat. I sucked air back into my lungs and then, for the second time in ten minutes, began to uncurl a corpse's fingers.

Before I got control of the steering, we scraped against a DeSoto parked on the side of Fourteenth. Now, I steered with my torso supported by the top of the driver's seat and the cabby's doubled-over body. I pushed my shoes against the back seat to keep me steady. The cabby's foot resting on the gas pedal kept us going at over thirty miles per hour.

"They are coming, they are coming," Leontieva was roaring. "Not fast enough. Go faster."

She started climbing over the empty side of the front seat.

"Why aren't they firing anymore?" I shouted back.

"No need to waste bullets or alert the police. They will be alongside soon enough."

I glanced at the rearview mirror set in the dash. A dark Dodge coupe was flying along 150 yards behind us. For a fraction of a second I was back in a B-17 with a German fighter on my tail. Then Leontieva slipped next to me and the doubled-over dead cabby I lay on. She mashed her own nylon-covered left foot down on the dead man's work boot. The cab lurched forward.

"You need to turn at P Street," she called.

"What?"

"Make a right here."

The tires shrieked in protest as I twisted the wheel. "We are going too fast," I shouted. She slid down and reached the brake with her foot, which helped some, but not enough. I scraped the bumper off a parked car before I could straighten out the cab.

"Up ahead is Dupont Circle. We'll pick up New Hampshire there," she directed.

I ran the light on Seventeenth and came within inches of a two-tone Pontiac driven by a matron dressed in her Sunday best. Mouthing a "fuck you," she slammed on the brakes and skidded to a stop in the middle of the intersection. Through the mirror I watched the Dodge clip its front and spin it around like a watch's second hand. We gained a few yards.

"We need to push this guy over," I called to Leontieva.

She understood what I meant and slid the cabby against the driver door as I swung my legs from the backseat. She ducked and I was seated behind the wheel. I kicked the cabby's boot out of my way.

Now I could drive. I was back in the pilot's seat where I belonged. We entered Dupont Circle going over fifty.

We whirled around the ring that surrounded a leafy oasis with a marble fountain in its center. Who the hell was Dupont anyway? I split a gap between two cars. I scraped one and then bounced off the other. They put on their brakes. Good. More beached whales for the Dodge to avoid.

Following Leontieva's directions, I swung the car out of the circle at New Hampshire Avenue. I crossed the median and passed cars on my right. Crossing O Street, we were tearing ass, going sixty. My head hit the car ceiling as we dipped into a pothole. In the mirror I could see the Dodge coming on to New Hampshire. It barreled into a pedestrian, who went flying. By M Street they were seventy-five yards and one Buick station wagon behind us. That hit pedestrian gave me an idea. I slowed the cab.

"Take the wheel," I yelled, and Leontieva closed the fingers of her left hand around it.

I pulled up on the door handle and swung the door open. "Sorry, fella," I muttered. With both hands I pushed the cabby's body out of the car. The same right foot that had stubbornly stayed on the accelerator got caught on the door frame. The corpse's skull was thudding along New Hampshire Avenue. I kicked at his boot, once, twice, three times before it let go. I jerked the door closed with one last apology and looked into the rearview mirror in time to see the station wagon between the deadly Dodge and us brake and then swerve to avoid the cabby's corpse. Two seconds later the Dodge slammed into its rear with a satisfying squeal of tires and crash of metal and glass.

Chapter Twenty-Nine

I had the wheel again and slowed as we approached Washington Circle.

"Your second right is Pennsylvania," my tourist guide, Miss Leontieva, said.

Now I heard sirens behind us. God, I hoped the D.C. police were ready for GRU gunmen.

As I entered the Circle and passed Twenty-third, the sirens were screeching louder. I looked to my right. A hundred yards up the street was a squad car, red light flashing, coming after us.

"How much further?" I shouted.

"One block."

I pushed down on the gas and turned hard on to Pennsylvania. Shit. I swung up on the sidewalk to miss a couple of college-aged kids walking arm in arm. I had the steering wheel to hold me down, but this time it was Leontieva's head that hit the roof. "Oof."

Halfway down the block, a barricade of white trestles was set up. I hit the brakes. As we emerged from the taxi, a D.C. police car pulled up twenty feet behind us. Two cops opened its doors and shouted for us to put our hands up. With their guns out they felt no need to say please.

I looked around. On the other side of the barricade were more uniforms unholstering their weapons.

Well, we sure as hell weren't going to make it the half block to the church by making a run for it.

I raised my hands over my head and Leontieva followed my lead.

The two D.C. policemen came out from behind the shield of their car doors with guns drawn.

When they were within ten feet, I said, "I'm Nate Michaels. I need to talk to the President."

"I don't think so, buster," said one of them.

"I have my White House I.D. in my wallet." I started to reach for it.

"Keep your hands up or I shoot."

I put my hands back up.

One of the officers approached with handcuffs.

"Listen," I screamed. "This is life-and-death. Millions of lives."

The cop's reply was to snap the cuffs around my wrists.

"You're coming with us."

He grabbed the chain between the cuffs and dragged me to the car while his partner showed a little more courtesy to Miss Leontieva. She was being guided by her arm. Appearances could be deceptive. She was far more dangerous than I.

"Call the White House," I said.

"And they'll say it's okay to kill a cabby and steal his cab?" the officer said. His hand was pushing my head down and into the back seat.

"There's a car with GRU gunmen back there on New Hampshire. They're killers."

"GRU? What the hell is GRU?"

He slammed the door shut and then Leontieva was next to me and the other door slammed.

I looked down at myself. I wasn't sure which of the bloodstains on my shirt and pants were from Volkov and which from the cabby.

In any case I didn't look ready for church with anyone, let alone the president.

"They will let you out when they find out who you are, *nyet*?" she asked.

"After World War III starts, who cares?"

Chapter Thirty

The two policemen climbed into the front seat. As they started to pull away, a man in a gray suit appeared in front of the car and waved his arms.

The car stopped, and the driver opened the door. The man in front of the car flicked open his wallet. "Agent Christian, Secret Service."

"What is it?" the D.C. cop asked.

Christian stuck his head in and looked at me. "Yes, what is it, Mr. Michaels?"

"Glad to see you again, Agent Christian. We need to talk to the President *now*."

"He's in church."

"Now," I said.

"Where are Kalinsky and Stewart?" Christian asked.

"The agents? Dead. Killed. By the GRU."

He pulled a walkie-talkie off his belt.

"Where?"

"House at 1448 Swann."

He was still speaking into the mike when we stopped in front of the church at a small gap in a second set of barricades.

St. Stephen Martyr Church was not the Gothic edifice I expected. In front of a modern brick building soared a fifty-foot concrete bell tower crowned by a cross.

"What's up, George?" the navy-suited agent asked Christian.

"Len, Mr. Michaels and his associate need to get in to see the President."

"Who is Mr. Michaels?" The agent called Len spoke as if I weren't there.

"An assistant to the president."

"The president is in there. Services." He ran his eyes over my blood-spattered clothing.

"Mr. Michaels says it's life or death."

"Life or death," I echoed.

"Okay if you say so, George," Len said. "They need to be patted down, though. It'll take a few minutes to find a matron for her." He jerked his head toward Leontieva.

"Just do it," she said with a roll of the eyes.

Christian patted her down and Len me. When Christian hesitated at her split skirt, she pulled the front flap up to reveal the tops of her nylons, a black garter belt, and two strips of milk-white flesh in between. He gave a quick peek and signaled for her to let the skirt down. He was blushing.

Len finished running his hands over my jacket and pants. "You're going into the church looking like that?" he asked.

I didn't answer. Christian, Leontieva, and I walked into St. Stephen Martyr Church through arched wooden doors set in the brick. The back of the church was dark. A few agents and a uniformed man stood back there. I went up to the open doors and looked into the nave. While the concrete and brick exterior gave the church the feeling of a factory building, the inside soared. The ceiling spread white plaster wings over the worshippers. A circular stained glass window with a lamb in the middle diffused the colors of the rainbow over a huge cross with the body of Christ hanging, stigmata visible even from where I stood.

The president was walking away from the priest in front. He must have just taken communion. Others were still in line as the priest slipped wafers into the mouths of each person who came before him. Kennedy probably hadn't even had time to swallow his.

Before he sat down in his pew, the third one back, he looked up. He raised his eyebrows in inquiry. I nodded a yes.

I watched him come up the aisle, leaning forward in his bad-back walk. Dave Powers followed.

Kennedy looked me up and down.

"Are you all right?"

"People are dead."

"From the looks of you, you came close to martyrdom yourself," he said.

"This is Miss Leontieva from the Russian Embassy," I said.

The president nodded at her and asked me, "What you got?"

I reached into my pants pocket and extracted the flimsy sheet of paper I'd taken out of Volkov's dead hand. "A message from Moscow," I answered.

"When was this sent?" he asked.

I looked down at my watch. Ten thirty. Amazing. Only 45 minutes had gone by since Volkov had offered me a cigar.

"I was there when it came in on shortwave less than an hour ago."

He handed the slip back to me. "So what does it say?"

I, in turn, handed it to Leontieva.

She translated, "U.S. guarantees no invasion of Cuba and takes missiles out of Turkey within five months as planned. USSR withdraws missiles and specialists from Cuba. Peace-loving USSR avoids war that would kill millions. Sent with approval of Nikita Sergeyevich. S."

"I told them we would not boast of victory," I told Jack.

"Who is S?" he asked Leontieva.

"A close aide of the First Secretary," she said.

"Like maybe the head of the KGB?" I asked.

She shrugged.

"You're sure about this, Nate?"

"Yes. Volkov sent the message, and this was the reply. It's in his own handwriting."

"Where is he now?"

"Dead. GRU."

"I'm sorry. Too many martyrs." He turned and looked at Christ on the cross. "We don't need any more." I knew he was thinking of the last world war and the next one. He turned around. "Dave, find Bobby. We'll need him to see Dobrynin."

He looked down at his watch and beckoned to a military aide in an air force uniform carrying a briefcase. Was this the man with the football? Did the case hold launch codes? "Major, tell General LeMay to call back the planes. Right now. We have twenty minutes before they enter Cuban airspace. Tell him the order comes from me."

"Yes, sir." He saluted but I might have seen a muscle under his eye twitch. Even with Kennedy's addendum, I didn't envy that officer's assignment.

"Let's go back in there," the president said.

I looked down at my clothes that bore evidence of two deaths.

"Look at my pants. It's not appropriate for me to be in church," I said.

"Take a look at Jesus on the cross." Kennedy pointed. "Plenty of blood in the sanctuary already. And you, Miss Leontieva, would you like to join us?"

"No, I must go back to the Soviet Embassy. It will be safe now."

"George, please get Miss Leontieva a ride."

I extended my hand to her. "Thank you. Volkov would be proud of what you've done. You are a brave woman.

"If you were Russian, you'd get a medal. You'd be named Hero of the Soviet Union," she told me.

During the War, I'd received a Distinguished Flying Cross. Anyone who made it to his thirtieth mission received one. I hadn't felt heroic when the general pinned it on my tunic. The medal meant I'd survived, nothing more. My citation was a mimeograph with my name filled in by a typewriter with a worn-out ribbon. Chasing through the streets of Washington in a taxi wasn't the same as flying over Germany in a B-17, but in both cases I'd done as directed and ended up surprised to be alive, surprised my allotment of luck hadn't run out.

Leontieva gave my hand a businesslike squeeze and Kennedy and I watched her walk out of the church, shoeless but dignified.

Then, heedless of blood and grime, the president swung an arm encased in Savile Row chalk stripes around my shoulder and walked me back to his pew.

As we sat down, he whispered to me, "So here I am praying to the Father, the Son, and the Holy Ghost to keep war from coming. And then you show up with this message? How do you figure?"

Chapter Thirty-One

By Eleven thirty I was back in the Cabinet Room, unshowered but in clean clothes.

"This came in from the Foreign Broadcast Information Service," McGeorge Bundy said, waving what looked like a telegram. "Radio Moscow just broadcast a message from Khrushchev to President Kennedy stating that the USSR had decided to dismantle Soviet missiles in Cuba and return them to the Soviet Union."

A cheer went up around the table.

Bundy then swept his eyes around the table. He wasn't done. "Everyone knows who were the hawks and who were the doves over the last two weeks. Today is the doves' day."

A gracious statement from the main spokesman on the ExComm for the hawks.

Then Bobby entered the room.

"What did Dobrynin have to say, Bobby?" his brother asked.

His toothy smile was answer enough, but words completed the report. "The ambassador conveyed his government's intention to withdraw the missiles and bombers and he passed on the First Secretary's best wishes to you, Mr. President."

"Good work. We've been lied to before by the Russians, and we'll need to have reconnaissance flights to confirm the dismantling of the missile sites. Maybe the United Nations can do that. Not today, though. And now this next point." Kennedy turned around and looked at me for a moment. "We won. We are getting the missiles out. But we could still lose. How? By boasting that we won. We need to be reserved in our comments. Pierre, I want you to tell the networks not to play up the story as a victory for us. Khrushchev could be so humiliated and angered he could change his mind like that." Kennedy snapped his fingers.

"Now, Dean, we could use the complete transcript of what Radio Moscow said. Then I could use some help in drafting a response to Khrushchev."

The meeting broke up. Kennedy looked at Bobby and then me and we followed him down the hall into his office.

Kennedy climbed onto his rocker and leaned it back. "Thank God. I feel like a new man." He reached for a cigar and offered us one. Bobby declined. This time I lit one up, for Volkov.

"So what should we do to mark the occasion?" Kennedy asked.

I puffed. "This is a pretty good cigar," I said.

"Here's what I was thinking," he continued. "Right after Lee surrendered, Lincoln wanted to celebrate his moment of triumph by going to the theater."

"So he went to Ford's Theater to see a production of 'Our American Cousin,'" Bobby said.

"Right. I should go to the theater tonight," Kennedy said.

Bobby at first seemed unsure how to react to this macabre line of reasoning. Then he opted for fraternal solidarity. "If you go, I'll go with you."

Kennedy laughed. "Listen, we'd be at war if it weren't for you two. Thank you."

"It was Volkov. A brave man. Khrushchev too," I said. "His move took guts. Before he died, Volkov predicted Khrushchev's reward for stopping war would be loss of power."

"Serves him right," Bobby said. "If he hadn't tried to sneak the missiles in, we'd all be better off."

"We'll see," the president said. He leaned back in his rocker and took a long puff. He exhaled with a sigh. After the last tendril of smoke floated up from his mouth, he said, "We make a good team and need to keep it together. We'll have a dinner tonight. I'll get Jackie back here. Just a few of us. We'll kick back and celebrate. That's what we'll do."

I spent the next hour explaining first to the president and attorney general and then to the FBI and CIA what I'd been doing that morning. They had a lot of cleaning up to do.

After I was done, I called Western Union and sent a telegram to the hotel in Mendocino telling my wife and kids they should go home.

Chapter Thirty-Two

I sat back in my coach seat in the darkened cabin of the 707, staring at the ceiling.

"You don't want to watch the movie?"

I jerked and saw a navy-uniformed stewardess leaning over me. The spool of film that had been playing in my mind broke. A bullet had just smashed into Volkov's head.

"Huh?"

"You don't want to watch the movie?" she repeated with a smile. Each word she spoke pushed the cinnamon scent of her Dentyne my way.

On the pull-down screen five rows ahead, colored images of Cary Grant and Doris Day were prancing around. A real movie, not an imaginary one.

"Oh, I saw it last summer," I said.

"Me too. You ever been on a plane with a movie before?"

"Nope. Fine for the passengers, but you must get tired of watching it over and over."

"I'll say. You're the only passenger not watching. Can I get you anything? A drink? Peanuts?"

"Thank you, no."

"What a relief," she said. She ran the back of her hand across her forehead. There was no real perspiration there, but she did knock her perky, French beret–inspired cap askew.

"I beg your pardon?"

"Cuba. No war. What a relief." She pantomimed the gesture of relief again and knocked the cap all the way off.

I caught it off the armrest and handed it to her. "It sure is."

The tinny voice of the pilot came over the speakers to tell us we were crossing the Mississippi. Three hours to go.

I hadn't come to Washington out of any personal loyalty to Jack Kennedy.

I'd walked out of the White House at three on that Sunday afternoon and this time the Secret Service hadn't stopped me. As I trod down the driveway, a caravan of black cars had entered the gate. Jackie Kennedy and the two kids were in the second one.

She'd lowered the window and gestured for me to come over. I could see the two children sleeping on the seat. I put my hands on the opening.

"Little angels," I said.

"Thank you for coming back here and helping Jack," she said in the half-whisper that was her speaking voice. "I know what it cost you."

"When others lost their heads, Jack kept his. A great man," I said.

"A great man, a good father, and my husband for better or worse," she said.

We both knew that being close to him extracted a heavy price.

She stuck her head out the car window, dragged me down to her, and kissed my cheek. As the car pulled away, she waved.

I walked the block over to the Willard Hotel to pick up a taxi. The driver turned on the radio at my request, and I caught the CBS hourly news at three. No boasting? George Herman described the resolution of the crisis as a humiliating setback for the Soviets. That wouldn't help Khrushchev any. The local news led with a report about a gas explosion on Swann Street Northwest that had left four residents and two passersby dead.

The cab pulled up to the curb at National at 3:25. I ran to the TWA ticket counter where I managed to wrangle an aisle seat on the day's last nonstop to San Francisco International. Jack would know why I'd left without saying goodbye. He'd know why I didn't want to join his team.

The seats were a lot more comfortable and the jet engines propelled the plane across the continent a lot faster, but I had the same feeling I'd had back in 1945. Another war was over and I was coming home for better or worse. Redemption – again.

The 707 took off at four and landed five and a half hours later. I had the time change working for me – the cab from the airport dropped me off at home before seven thirty. The family had made it back from Mendocino. The boys spotted me through the picture window and came out shouting like banshees as I handed the driver a ten-dollar bill for the ride. I told him to keep the change.

Under the streetlamp in front of the house, they made what they called a "Dad Sandwich," one on each side, their arms around me squeezing like pythons. Although only sixteen, both boys were the same six feet I was. Judging from the pressure on my ribcage, they were at least as strong too.

"Can we go car-shopping tomorrow, Dad?"

"Yeah, sure," I said.

Then my wife was a shadow standing in the front doorway, backlit by the foyer's chandelier. I could see a silhouetted hand go up to her mouth. A moment later, her feet were drumming down the bricks of the walkway.

Then I had a third pair of arms encircling me.

"We watched the news. You're all done back there?" she asked.

"Thanks to you."

"You're home with me, with us, for good?"

I was done, wasn't I? No more unfinished business with Kennedy or from the War.

"Yes."

She pulled my head down and pushed my lips against hers. The boys groaned in teenaged mortification.

I closed my eyes.

Here I was back home again with my children, my future, and the only woman I'd ever wanted.

I opened my eyes and looked at her.

Miriam.

THE END

Acknowledgments

Once I learned that future president John F. Kennedy had spent the fall quarter of 1940 at Stanford, a historical thriller was the inevitable result. I'm not sure why this episode of a life so well-documented remains so little-known today. As a boy growing up in Palo Alto, I ate with my parents at L'Omelette and pedaled my bike past Hoover Tower, never suspecting I was so close to JFK's old haunts.

I did my best to fit the events of this book into the interstices of the historical record. A shelf at home bows beneath the weight of memoirs, biographies, and histories covering the events and characters I've written about. Of all the sources consulted, five were particularly valuable and deserve mention. First is *The Kennedy Tapes: Inside the White House During the Cuban Missile Crisis*, some 500 pages of word-for-word transcriptions of the ExComm deliberations. This volume was co-edited by the late Ernest May, one of the great historians of the last century and a favorite professor of mine in college. Bert Stiles gave me a sense of what it meant to be a B-17 pilot in the stark, moving, and cynical language of his memoir *Serenade to the Big Bird*. But like Anne Frank, Stiles remained an idealist amidst the slaughter. And like Anne Frank again, Stiles did not survive the war. I wore out a copy of *Designing Camelot: The Kennedy White House Restoration* by James Abbot and Elaine Rice, opening it again and again to ensure accurate descriptions of White House rooms and the labyrinthine passages between them. The letters, notes, clippings, and papers archived in the Kennedy Presidential Library in Boston provided an invaluable insight into JFK as a young man and as president. My daughter Maddie, who helped me go through the materials, especially relished seeing the 35th president's not-so-stellar Harvard report cards. Last, Mary Liz McCurdy opened the archives of *The Stanford Daily* to me. Reading those old papers provided a sense of being right there on campus with JFK, Nate, and Miriam in October 1940.

When I told old college pal Rick Wolff that JFK's presence at Stanford would be the jumping-off point for my next novel, he suggested I find a tie-in with the Cuban Missile Crisis. The versatile Maddie Raffel served as a nonpareil research assistant, editor, and literary advisor. A line-up of the usual suspects, a group near and dear to me that includes Wes Raffel, Dena Raffel, Corey Raffel, Loren Saxe, Josh Getzler, and Larry Vincent, gave me their usual insightful suggestions and much-needed encouragement during the writing of the book. The oh-so talented writers Seth Harwood, L.J. Sellers, Boyd Morrison, and Sean Chercover provided wise counsel and support, as did two dozen of my compadres who are members of the Killer Thrillers author collective. Masters of the thriller genre like William Martin, Steve Berry, Rebecca Cantrell, Robert Gregory Browne, Kelli Stanley, and Gayle Lynds took time to write about this book in words so generous they make me blush. I must (grudgingly) admit to owing Marcus Sakey big time for his friendship, support, and ingenious conniving. Any author would be proud to have readers like Kevin Compton, Lynn Hirshman, Cathi Thoorsell, Ivan Kolaszvari, and Josh Parker who, lucky for me, do not keep their opinions to themselves. As always, the team at Quattro supplied me with the unfailing hospitality and rivers of green tea that made their café a perfect oasis for writing this book.

Everyone I dealt with at Thomas & Mercer has acted in a manner both decisive and supportive. I am thrilled and delighted to have this book published by them. Thank you so much to Anh Schluep for believing in *A Fine and Dangerous Season*. It's been a pleasure. Kudos to Jacque BenZekry and Tiffany Pokorny for their marketing savvy and responsiveness. Thank you also to Jennifer McIntyre for the sharpness of eye and ear that she brought to bear in her editing. And to Dale Roberts and Travis Young for the artistic flair they showed in cover design.

Of course, without the support of my wife and children, neither this book nor any of my others would have been written. Heartfelt thanks to the five of them for tolerating the eccentric author in their midst.

I am so grateful to all these friends, colleagues, and family members who made writing this book such a fun and fulfilling endeavor.

Keith Raffel,
Palo Alto, California

About the Author

Born in Chicago, Keith Raffel has lived in Palo Alto since he was eight. As a boy growing up there, he remembers eating with his parents at JFK's old haunts like L'Omelette, long gone, and selling soft drinks at football games at Stanford Stadium, since rebuilt. He watched as local orchards filled with cherry and apricot trees were replaced by tilt-up buildings filled with software engineers and MBAs. He founded UpShot Corporation, Silicon Valley's first cloud-computing company, which won numerous awards. In addition to his career as an entrepreneur, Keith has been counsel to the Senate Intelligence Committee, a college writing instructor at Harvard, a candidate for Congress in California's 12th District, a professional gambler at Bay Area horse tracks, and chief commercial officer at a DNA sequencing company. (He seems to have career ADD, doesn't he?) An avid reader of crime fiction since picking up his first *Hardy Boys* mystery, Keith became a published author in 2006 with *Dot Dead*, which Bookreporter.com called "the most impressive mystery debut of the year." These days he stays busy following the San Francisco Giants and writing his novels just around the block from where he grew up.